CREATIVE WOMAN MYSTERIES®

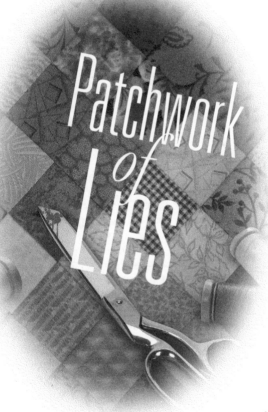

Patchwork of Lies

Sharon Dunn

Annie's®
AnniesFiction.com

Books in the Creative Woman Mysteries series

Library of Congress-in-Publication Data
Patchwork of Lies / by Sharon Dunn
p. cm.
I. Title
                    2013906454

AnniesFiction.com
800-282-6643
Creative Woman Mysteries®
Series Editor: Shari Lohner

10 11 12 13 14 | Printed in China | 9 8 7 6 5

1

Shannon McClain awoke to the sound of a burglary in progress. After a long morning of helping her friend Betty Russo get ready for an onslaught of guests at The Apple Grove Inn, she had lain on the couch in the little room used to store furniture next to the inn's office. She'd only intended to rest her eyes. Instead, she'd fallen into a deep sleep. A full day of getting everything organized for the quilting workshops Betty planned to facilitate during the Apple Festival had left Shannon exhausted.

At first, still in a groggy state, Shannon couldn't comprehend what the odd scratching and thumping sounds in the room next to her meant. She opened her eyes, straining to hear through the wall. A drawer slid open and slammed shut. She sat up, wondering if Tom and Betty had returned home early from grocery shopping.

As she listened to someone banging around in the office, the hairs on the back of her neck prickled. Instinctively she knew it wasn't Tom or Betty.

Shannon rose from the sofa, treading lightly across the carpeted floor. She eased the door open. A narrow sliver of the office came into view as the noise, stomping and a rapid opening and closing of drawers, increased in intensity.

Her breath caught in her throat.

She saw broad shoulders and a dark hood drawn up over

the head—probably a man. With his back turned to her, the intruder rifled through file cabinet drawers.

Shannon pushed the door fully open and stood paralyzed as her heart thumped a mile a minute. *What can I do?* She'd left her cellphone in another room. The office phone rested only inches away from where the man frantically searched through drawers.

Steeling herself against her rising fear, she cleared her throat. In the strongest voice she could manage, she said, "What are you doing in here?"

The man turned, his head bent down. He bolted toward the door. On instinct, Shannon stepped forward to block his escape. He barreled into her, knocking her to the floor. Stunned from the impact, it took her a moment to recover. As she scrambled to her feet, she heard the back door open and slam shut. She raced after the intruder.

She struggled to catch her breath as she searched the trees behind the inn and surrounding property. No sign of the man. No one sitting on the patio chairs. The few guests who were already checked in were probably napping in their rooms or had gone into town. Shannon turned, pressing her hand against her back where it had impacted with the floor. It hurt every time she inhaled.

She hurried back to the office. Her hand shook as she picked up the phone to call Chief Grayson.

"Apple Grove police, Chief Grayson speaking."

She pressed the phone hard against her ear. "Chief, it's Shannon McClain. I'm over at The Apple Grove Inn." She couldn't hide the tremble in her voice.

"Shannon, has something happened?"

The commanding strength of Grayson's voice calmed her nerves. "Someone broke into the Russos' office. I caught him in the act, but he got away."

"How long ago did this happen?"

"Not more than five minutes ago." Shannon paused for a breath, still winded from the pursuit.

"Which way did he run?" Grayson's voice remained steady.

Shannon turned in a semicircle and gazed at the door that led to the patio. "He ran out the back door, toward the grove of trees behind the inn."

"Tell me anything you can remember about what he looked like."

She closed her eyes. Her heart had slowed down to near normal, but her hands still vibrated. "Ummm ... I didn't get a look at his face. He wore a dark hoodie pulled up over his head."

"I'll send an officer to search the area and the streets on the other side of those trees. And Shannon, you sit tight. I'll be right over." Compassion filled his voice.

"Thank you."

After placing the phone in its cradle, Shannon collapsed into the office chair. As she sat studying the open drawers and scattered papers, she noticed a foreign scent lingering in the air. She breathed more deeply, realizing that the distinct woodsy smell had been most intense when the intruder had knocked her over. *It must be the burglar's cologne.*

At the sound of a siren, she leaped to her feet and headed toward the front of the inn. Betty and Tom's sedan pulled into the driveway just ahead of the police SUV. Betty pushed the passenger side door open and stepped toward the inn, holding a bag of groceries. The stiffness in her stride indicated that her arthritis might be acting up. She glanced at the police vehicle and then at Shannon, her eyes growing wide with unspoken questions.

Shannon swooped down the steps and put an arm around her friend. "I caught a man in your office. I tried to stop him." She managed to keep her voice calm.

Betty let out a sharp breath. She touched her palm to her chest.

Tom skirted the front of the car to stand beside his wife. "We were robbed?" He gripped the bag of groceries tighter.

"He opened a bunch of drawers. I'm not sure if he took anything." The look of shock on Tom and Betty's faces crushed Shannon. If only she had anticipated being knocked over, she might have been able to catch the guy.

Chief Grayson opened his SUV door. His boots pounded the concrete as he lumbered toward them. "Why don't we go inside and talk?"

"I'll take care of the groceries, Bets." Tom took the bag from Betty and disappeared inside.

Shannon squeezed Betty's shoulder in a sideways hug and led her up the stairs. They stepped into the lobby with Chief Grayson taking up the rear.

Grayson shoved his hands into his pockets, glancing around the lobby and into the empty tearoom. "Quiet this time of day."

Betty responded after a moment, a dazed look in her eyes. "I wanted the place mostly empty today, so it would be easier to get it ready for the big crowd coming in." She combed her fingers through her curly auburn hair. "With the Apple Festival starting tomorrow, we'll be full up by tonight. People made reservations months ago."

"The office is on the far side of the inn, away from the guest rooms," Shannon said as she treaded across the plush carpet.

"What were you doing here, Shannon?" Grayson paced the lobby, running his hand over the back of a Victorian-style couch done in a rich floral fabric. "With all the craft vendors in the park and everything else going on for the festival, I'd think you'd be plenty busy at the Paisley Craft Market."

Shannon stopped and turned to face Grayson. "We are very busy at my store." The whole town buzzed in anticipation of the festival. "But Betty needed to do a lot of extra preparation for the workshops, so I offered to help her out."

Though she'd only lived in Apple Grove a short time, Shannon felt a strong loyalty to Betty. Betty had been the first person in Apple Grove to befriend her after she'd traveled all the way from Wainscott, Scotland, to claim her inheritance from her grandmother—a mansion with a summer house and the craft market. Despite the fact that they'd never met, Victoria Paisley had been generous to her granddaughter.

The chief turned toward Betty, now seated on a couch in the lobby. The worry lines on her forehead intensified. "Betty, I'm going to need your input too," he said. "Perhaps you can help us figure out what the intruder took or what he meant to steal. Try not to disturb anything. We'll get a deputy over here to dust for prints."

Betty managed a nod, though the dazed expression of stunned disbelief remained. Once they entered the office,

Shannon talked the police chief through what had happened. She strode across the room, pointing out where she'd been standing when the intruder knocked her over.

"I wonder what he wanted in here." Grayson put his beefy hands on his police utility belt and turned to Shannon. "Did you notice if he held anything as he ran away?"

Shannon closed her eyes and pictured the thief barreling toward her. *Was anything in his hands?* It had all happened so fast. She shook her head. "I'm not sure."

Betty wandered around the room, growing paler by the minute. Her hand covered her mouth as her eyes glazed.

Shannon's heart broke over what her friend must be feeling. This couldn't be easy for her.

Betty gazed at the papers flung all over the floor, the open photo album on the desk, and the gaping drawers. "It doesn't look like anything is missing." She peered inside one of the drawers. "The petty cash box is still here."

An image flashed through Shannon's head of the thief shoving something into his pocket. Could she trust her memory? "He might have taken something small; I'm not sure what."

Tom poked his head into the room, his dark eyes filled with concern. "Groceries are all put away." He stepped toward his wife. "Why don't you lie down for a rest if you're done in here?"

"Oh, Tom, I don't know if I can. I've got so much to do before the guests arrive." Betty wrung her hands. "My list of last-minute things to get together for the workshops is a mile long." She looked around at the scattered papers. "And now I have this mess to deal with." Tears formed in her eyes.

"You'll have to leave this untouched until we can go

over it." Grayson smoothed a hand over his bald spot.

Tom wrapped his arms around Betty, his large frame enveloping her. "A short rest will do you good." He led her out of the room. Normally a gregarious man, especially around guests, Tom now displayed a much softer, caring side. No wonder their marriage had lasted more than thirty years.

The chief waited to talk to Shannon until Betty and Tom had left the room. "So you think he took something?"

"I think he put something either in a pocket or inside his coat." Shannon surveyed the room. The petty cash lay untouched in an open drawer. A framed set of collector coins hung on the wall, seemingly undisturbed. *What did the thief intend to steal?*

Grayson leaned toward her. "I see your mind racing a hundred miles an hour." He raised his eyebrows in a show of reprimand. "Leave the detective work to my deputies and me."

Shannon sighed. "Sorry." She couldn't help it if her natural curiosity took over. Besides, she wanted to help her friend.

"The one way I do want you to help is to tell me if you think you could identify him. I know you said you didn't see his face, but take a moment. Was there anything distinct about the guy?"

"He had a hood on, and he kept his head bent down the whole time." She certainly couldn't remember what he looked like when he had charged at her. "However, his cologne smelled really unique. I'd recognize the smell anywhere."

The chief furled his forehead, and the corners of his mouth turned up. "I don't think there has ever been a police lineup based on smell."

Shannon laughed and put her hands over her face.

"Sorry—just trying to remember every detail, anything that might help us catch him." The brief exchange of humor lightened the moment for both of them.

The chief hiked up his belt. "You mean anything that would help *the police* catch him?"

"Yes, of course." Shannon smiled innocently.

"I've got a deputy out searching the area. I'll radio him. If he hasn't found anything, he can drive over to dust for prints and process the scene. With all the guests they're expecting, I'm sure Betty and Tom will need to use the office."

Shannon followed Grayson out to the great room. "I'll let you know if I remember anything else that might be helpful."

"Good. I'll have my officer over here as soon as possible." With a clipped nod, Grayson headed out the door.

Shannon listened to the rumble of his SUV as it pulled out of the driveway. When she walked past the sunroom, she noticed Betty, setting out quilt samples.

"Did you decide not to take that nap?"

Betty shook her head. "I still need the fabric samples from your shop and the beads for the class you're going to teach." She spoke at a rapid pace.

"I can bring those by later today." Shannon unfolded a quilted lap blanket and searched for a place to display it. She found herself wanting to offer words of comfort but unsure of what to say. A break-in like this could make Betty fearful it might happen again—Shannon knew from experience.

Betty bustled around the room, placing quilts over chairs and arranging blocks of fabric on a table. She seemed to be dealing with her emotions by staying busy. "I think this room will be a good place to display things," she said. "If people want to set up quilt projects between classes, they can do it here. This area is really conducive to people visiting with one another while they're working on their projects."

"It sounds like you've thought of everything. I'm sure the guests are going to have a wonderful time."

Betty hadn't stopped moving since Shannon entered the room. Now she rearranged the sample quilt blocks for the third time. "Make sure you remind Deborah to call and let me know exactly what she's covering in her classes, will you? Oh, and she promised she'd bring her quilt frame over."

Deborah Waters, Shannon's cook and an expert quilter, had also been her grandmother Victoria's cook and confidant. "I'll remind her, but I'm sure she's on top of all that."

"I can't tell you how much your coming over has helped me." Betty stopped flitting around the room and looked directly at Shannon, her blue eyes shining with gratitude.

"I'm glad to do it."

"My only sister died when I was young. I can't help but think that if she had lived, she would have been a lot like you." Betty's voice was thick with emotion.

The compliment floored Shannon. "I'm so honored you said that."

"I know you must have a ton of things to do at the craft market, but you chose to help me instead. That means a lot to me."

The decision to help Betty prepare the inn for the workshops had meant work would pile up at Shannon's shop. But it had been worth it to spend time with Betty. Essie Engleman, the manager of the Paisley Craft Market &

Artist Lofts, could handle most of the tasks at the shop, and Shannon had hired a high school girl, Kristin O'Connor, to help out during the busy festival. "It was my pleasure. I just wish I could've caught that guy. I think he probably saw the two of you leave and assumed no one occupied that side of the inn."

Outside, the mail truck rumbled all the way up the long driveway.

"He must be bringing a package." Betty hurried across the room. "I hope it's the special preserves I ordered to serve at breakfast in the tearoom."

Shannon followed behind. Betty opened the door and disappeared outside. She returned with a box a moment later.

Shannon stared at the huge box. "How much jam did you order?"

"Not this much," Betty said. "This is too big to be six jars of marmalade."

Shannon retrieved scissors from the sunroom and handed them to Betty.

Betty checked the sides and the bottom of the box. "Strange. There's no return address."

The beat-up package didn't look like it had been wrapped by a business. Betty cut through the tape, folded the top flaps of the box down, and removed the tissue paper. With a gasp, she took a step back. "How could it be?" she whispered.

Shannon leaned forward and looked down at the folded quilt in the box. Betty's reaction told her it wasn't a sample quilt for the workshops.

Betty drew the quilt out of the box, revealing another

quilt beneath it. She held it to her chest, the look of shock on her face even more intense than when she'd learned of the robbery.

"Betty?"

Betty didn't respond. A faraway look formed in the older woman's eyes, now rimmed with tears.

Shannon smoothed her hand over the second quilt still in the box and said, "These hand-stitched quilts are beautiful." She cast a curious glance at Betty. "I wonder who sent them."

The question seemed to snap Betty out of her trance. She tossed the quilt on the floor and wiped at the corner of her eyes. "It doesn't matter."

"But you *do* know who they came from."

"It doesn't make any sense," Betty muttered. She picked up the box and dropped it carelessly by the fireplace. Without another word, she disappeared down the hallway.

Confused by her friend's odd behavior, Shannon listened to the hushed voices as Betty talked to Tom. Then she heard what sounded like crying.

Shannon kneeled down and picked up the quilt where Betty had tossed it. She folded it and carefully placed it in the box. Whoever made the quilts had demonstrated great skill. The quilter had created a pattern of two big stitches and one short stitch, so evenly done that it looked like machine work. The quilter had also incorporated bits of lace and embroidery into the pattern.

Shannon didn't know who the quilts might be from—or why Betty had reacted to them so strongly. But she understood one thing for sure: The arrival of the quilts had upset Betty far more than the break-in.

2

When the bell above the door at the Paisley Craft Market dinged for the umpteenth time, Shannon felt like she'd been tossed into a whirlwind. Flocks of tourists arriving early for the festival had crammed into the shop. She hadn't found a moment to catch her breath since leaving the inn.

Kristin, the high school girl she'd hired to help out at the store during the festival, approached Shannon as she merchandised the new cross-stitch books in the display racks. "I have a customer who wants to know if we have alpaca yarn."

"We don't carry that, but angora is also a really soft yarn and a great alternative." Shannon pointed toward the yarn selection. "Upper right-hand corner."

Kristin nodded and returned to an older woman waiting in the knitting area. The teenager seemed to be working out pretty well. She caught on quickly, and she asked for help when she needed it.

Essie Engleman, dressed in a flowing turquoise skirt and poet's blouse, buzzed past Shannon with two middle-aged women who sported T-shirts commemorating the Apple Festival trailing behind her. "Right this way, ladies." As always, Essie exuded boundless energy. Shannon couldn't have asked for a better manager.

Shannon placed the last pattern book on the rack,

a task she'd been trying to complete all day. With the extra customers in the store and all the interruptions, a task that would have normally taken twenty minutes had stretched out into late afternoon.

"Excuse me." A warm tenor voice caused her to turn. She saw a tall man with sandy blond hair standing in front of her. The deep tan of his skin hinted that he probably spent a great deal of time outside.

"Can I help you?" Shannon asked.

"I seem to be lost." He smiled, the corners of his dark green eyes crinkling. "This is obviously not the housing rental agency."

"That's on the other side of the street. Same block." Shannon straightened a row of fabric paints. "I take it you're not in town for the Apple Festival if you're looking for a place to rent."

"I'm a marine biologist, and I'm relocating to do some research." He indicated the crowds in the store and out on the street. "Looks like I picked the wrong week to move."

Shannon laughed. "Trust me; Apple Grove is usually a quiet little town. Things will be back to normal after the weekend. The festival lasts four days starting tomorrow, Wednesday through Saturday, with a few things going on Sunday morning. Welcome to our town. I'm Shannon McClain."

"Hunter Banks." He shook her hand with a firm grip.

"Maybe you'll have a chance to enjoy some of the fun in between your research. There's going to be a parade, craft vendors in the park, and a big concert on Saturday night, all part of the festival."

"I hope I do get the chance to enjoy some of it." The man tipped an imaginary hat to her. "I thank you for the directions." He sauntered out the door.

Nice guy.

A group of women, all dressed in yellow shirts and wearing red baseball caps, swarmed into the store. They made a beeline for Shannon, peppering her with questions.

"Is this where you get the Apple Festival buttons?"

"Do you have acrylic paints?"

"Where are baskets you can decorate?"

"What do you have that's on sale?"

Shannon answered the questions and directed the women to different parts of the store. From time to time, she observed Kristin's head bobbing up from the rest of the crowd while Essie darted between the cash register and the sales floor.

With all of the customers engaged, Shannon escaped and headed toward the storage room. She whizzed past Espresso Yourself, the store's coffee and tea bar, where the barista swirled whipped cream on a latte. Every table was occupied, with four customers waiting in line. Like the rest of the store, the coffee shop buzzed with activity.

Shannon stepped into the room where they kept merchandise ready to move out on the floor and closed the door. Some of the chatter from the main part of the store still reached her, but the room was definitely quieter. She needed a solitary place to collect her thoughts, and restocking inventory gave her the perfect excuse to linger in the quiet room. Thoughts about Betty and the arrival of the mysterious quilts still gnawed at her. She needed time to process it.

As she gathered a stack of the official Apple Festival T-shirts in her arms, she heard a light tapping on the door. Before she could answer, it swung open.

"Hey, kiddo." Joyce Buchanan poked her head in. "I saw you duck in here. No fair! You can't be hiding out." She held a brown paper bag with a grease stain on it. Shannon assumed it contained some delectable doughnut that Joyce had whipped up at her Pink Sprinkles Bakery.

"You're right." Shannon set the T-shirts to one side and pulled a box off the shelf. "I have to get a bunch of beads together to take over to Betty later." Her thoughts tangled like cheap yarn as she itemized everything she needed to do. "And then some of the artists who rent lofts upstairs have asked for my help moving their stuff to the booths at the park."

Joyce patted her platinum blond hair. "The bakery is swamped too. I think I've gotten two hours of sleep in the last three days thanks to all the extra baking. Once the tourists show up, anything edible flies off the shelves. Not that I'm complaining."

"Me either. Extra business is always nice." Shannon opened a box containing glass beads.

"Anyway," Joyce thrust the paper bag toward Shannon, "I thought you could use one of my special apple tarts."

Shannon took the bag. "You're a lifesaver. I haven't eaten since early this morning."

Joyce tossed her head and laughed, causing her long dangling earrings to swing. "So this is *just* what you need— a good old sugar rush."

Shannon clutched the bag to her chest. "Anything to keep me going."

"The Purls are still getting together at your house tomorrow night to work out a schedule for our booth—right?"

Shannon nodded. The Purls of Hope knitting circle, which consisted of Joyce, Betty, Melanie, Kate and herself, had decided to rent a booth at the park. They planned to sell their handicrafts, mostly knitted items, and donate the profits to cancer research. The women, known simply as the Purls, had welcomed Shannon into their ranks when she'd first arrived in Apple Grove, and now she considered them among her closest friends.

Shannon wondered how they would man the booth, what with Betty's workshops, the extra crowds at the stores, and everything else going on during the festival. "Hopefully we can manage to have someone at the booth in the park for most of the festival. I'm planning on doing the setup tomorrow, and Melanie said she could watch it for the day."

Joyce raised a well-groomed eyebrow. "This is your first Apple Festival, isn't it?"

"It is."

"You need to have a little fun then."

"I'll try. There's just so much work to do." Shannon considered telling Joyce about the break-in at Betty's inn and the mysterious quilts, but decided against it. Betty would share if she wanted to—assuming the Apple Grove rumor mill didn't spread the news first.

"I know. We're all busier than a long-tailed cat in a room full of rocking chairs," Joyce said. "Catch up with you later. I gotta get over to the bakery." She gave Shannon a hug before leaving.

Shannon closed the door, relishing the quiet. She

slipped the tart out of the bag and took a single bite of the luscious treat. The sweetness of the apples coated her tongue. Before she could fully savor it, another tap sounded at the door.

Matthew Conlin, a young sculptor who rented one of the lofts on the second floor of the craft market, stuck his head in. "Thought I might find you here."

So much for this being a great hiding place. "Hi, Matthew. What can I do for you?"

"Hate to bother you, but you said you'd give me a hand getting my stuff loaded to sell in the park." Matthew looked at his watch. "I don't have much time before I have to be back on the jobsite. My boss let me go for forty minutes."

Matthew earned his living as a master welder, and he put his skills to use creating sculptures from metal, rocks, and parts he found in junkyards.

Shannon picked up the box of beads she'd pulled earlier and the T-shirts. "Why don't you bring your van around to the alley? I think that would be the easiest way to get it loaded. Too much traffic on Main Street."

Matthew rubbed his chin and nodded. "Can't argue with you there, Mrs. M. This festival is going to be something else."

After dumping the box of beads and T-shirts onto the store counter, Shannon helped Matthew load his van with sculptures that varied in size from something a person could put on a coffee table to larger ones they had to transport with a hand truck.

"Thanks for your help, Mrs. M." Matthew wiped sweat from his brow. "After work tonight, I'm going to get the booth all put together. That way, all I have to do tomorrow morning is set up my merchandise now that it's all loaded."

His youthful enthusiasm and energy reminded Shannon of her son, Alec, who attended Portland State University. "That sounds like a good plan."

"I hope I make some money this weekend. I'm taking days off work to do this."

Matthew also demonstrated youthful insecurities similar to Alec's.

"You'll do great," she said, patting him on the back.

"This whole thing is pretty cool. I can't believe how many people are in town for it. I suppose a lot of it has to do with Angel Lewis headlining at the concert Saturday night," Matthew said, stepping toward his van and opening the door.

Shannon remembered seeing the posters advertising the concert. Angel Lewis had lived in Apple Grove as a teenager, and recently her song *Whirlwind* had hit the charts. The town council had shown enormous savvy in getting her to headline the concert. "I'm sure a lot of people your age are coming to see Angel. There's so much going on, I think we'll attract about every age group."

"It's going to be a great concert. Catch you later." Matthew climbed into his van and drove away.

Shannon assisted two other artists in loading their booths and handicrafts before her growling stomach drew her back to the storage room in search of her half-eaten tart. As her hand gripped the storage room doorknob, she noticed Michael Stone enter the shop. His blue gaze scanned the room, obviously looking for her.

Shannon's stomach coiled into a knot, but not from lack of food. Michael gave her whiplash where her emotions were concerned. She'd thought that he cared for her as more than a friend, and she'd allowed her heart to open up to the possibility—a big step after enduring the loss of her husband, John, more than three years ago. She'd never expected to have feelings of romantic affection for any man again. But just as her hope had risen to the surface, Michael had dashed it to pieces. He'd invited her to an event sponsored by his security company. When a criminal took advantage of the occasion to assault Michael, Shannon had ended up in the middle of the violence and had suffered a minor head injury. Everything had worked out OK, but Michael had never asked her out again. She knew why he'd closed himself off. He still blamed his dangerous line of work for his late wife's death, and he didn't want to put another woman in harm's way again. But it didn't make the situation any easier to accept.

Michael met her gaze and pushed through the crowd toward her.

Shannon planted her feet even as her stomach did somersaults. She was an adult. She could handle this.

"I heard about the burglary at the inn on the scanner," Michael said, his expression radiating warmth as he reached toward her. "Are you OK?"

His genuine concern helped her relax a little. "I'm fine. He knocked me over, but I sustained no injuries. What really bothers me is that the guy escaped. He's still out there."

"My men installed the security system at the inn. I'll make sure everything works like it should."

"I don't think the alarms were even on," she said. "The

thief must have seen Betty and Tom leave for the store and didn't realize I was still there."

"All the same, we want to make sure the Russos and their guests are safe." He rested his intense gaze on her, and a charge of electricity zinged through her body.

But at the same time, she retreated emotionally. He'd expressed as much concern over whether his alarm system had functioned correctly as he had for her. As a former cop who now ran a security company, Michael demonstrated an attitude of protectiveness toward almost everyone. She dared not interpret his fussing over her safety as romantic affection. That would only lead to more disappointment.

Brushing away the warm feelings, Shannon squared her shoulders and used her best businesslike voice. "Thanks for your concern. I'd better get to work. I've got a lot to do before the festival officially starts." She turned away from him, but she could still feel him watching her. Ignoring the unnerving sensation, she busied herself straightening some kids' craft kits which were already in perfect order.

When she turned around, she saw Michael making his way to the front of the store. The bells above the door jangled as he walked out the door.

Kristin joined her. "Mrs. McClain, my mom is here to pick me up." Kristin turned slightly and nodded at a blond woman wearing a shapeless yellow dress. "It's ten minutes earlier than we agreed on. I can stay if you need me to."

Shannon glanced at the clock. The store closed in less than an hour, but the customers kept crowding in. "You go ahead, honey. Maybe tomorrow you can stay until closing if you want to get some extra hours in."

Kristin clapped her hands together. "Oh, I'd love that!"

The thin woman in the yellow dress approached them. "Hi, I'm Sissy, Kristin's mom."

"Great news, Mom!" Kristin bounced. Her brown eyes filled with light. "Mrs. McClain is going to give me even more hours."

"We are much busier than I had anticipated," Shannon said.

Sissy grabbed Shannon's hand and patted it between hers. "I can't thank you enough for giving Kris this job." The woman's hands felt bony and dry. The deep furrows and wrinkles in her face spoke of a life of hard work. Though she couldn't be much older than Shannon, pronounced patches of gray streaked through her blond hair.

Shannon put her free hand over Sissy's. "I appreciate her help."

The sound of falling objects and several women exclaiming "Oh my!" near the front door drew Shannon away from the conversation. The window display, featuring stacked wooden boxes filled with various crafting tools, had crashed down and spilled out onto the floor.

"You'll have to excuse me." Shannon raced to the front of the store.

A woman with two young children clutching her skirt turned to Shannon. "I'm so sorry. I think Missy did that." She touched the head of one of the children. "Her curiosity got the better of her."

Missy hid half her face behind her mother's skirt. But Shannon could see the fear in the little girl's eyes. "It's all right. Accidents happen."

"If she broke anything, I'll pay for it," the woman offered.

Shannon shooed the idea away with her hand. "Don't worry about it. My kids are grown now and off to college, but I remember struggling to keep an eye on both of them while I tried to get my shopping done."

"Were your kids close in age?"

"Twins. A boy and a girl."

"Twins, how fun." The woman touched the heads of her little girls. "Missy and Angie are eighteen months apart."

Shannon's reassurances calmed the woman. She thanked Shannon again and headed toward the fabric section, her children in tow.

Shannon stepped up into the display window and proceeded to restack the boxes. As she carefully positioned the box that featured tools a knitter would use, a tapping at the window sounded. Startled, she turned to face the sidewalk.

Melanie Burkhart, another member of the Purls, stood outside on the sidewalk holding a small box. Her bright smile offset her dark hair. Delighted to see her friend, Shannon waved her in. A recent cancer survivor, Melanie was one of the reasons the Purls loved raising money for cancer research.

"You'll never believe what I have in here." Melanie held up the box. Her shoulders jerked up to her ears. "Go ahead and guess."

"A stuffed weasel," Shannon joked.

Melanie threw back her head and laughed. "Not hardly." She opened the box and pulled out a jar containing amber liquid. She unscrewed the jar's lid and tilted it toward Shannon. "What does that smell like?"

A heady fragrance filled the store. "Apple blossoms?"

The Apple Festival celebrated the harvest of the apples. Blossoms were long since gone.

Melanie nodded. "I'm in charge of decorating the float for the Apple Queen to ride on in the parade." Melanie utilized her knack for floral arrangement with her job at The Flower Pot. "I did a little research on perfumery and mixed the scent myself. This float is going to be a smell-o-rama experience."

"Impressive."

"The town council paid for tons of silk apple blossoms," Melanie said, twisting the lid on the jar. "Now all I have to do is attach them to the float. I've got a dispenser to spray the fake flowers with the scent."

"I can't wait to see it … and smell it."

Melanie placed the jar of perfume carefully in the box. "You've had quite a busy day. I heard about the robbery at the inn. How's Betty doing?"

"I think she's pretty upset." Shannon's thoughts turned to her friend. Even though the break-in had clearly shaken Betty up, her strong reaction to the arrival of the quilts took prominence in Shannon's mind. *Melanie's known Betty longer than I have; maybe she'd know what the mystery quilts are about.* She opened her mouth to ask, but then thought better of it. The quilts obviously reminded Betty of something painful. Perhaps it was best to keep the matter private. If Betty wanted to share anything with the other Purls, she would. "I know we're all really busy, but if you think of it, you might want to give her a call or swing by."

Melanie nodded. "I'll do my best. I've got to drop off

flowers for the tearoom. I'll try to catch her then. Gotta run." She rolled her eyes. "We're probably going to be working through the night on this float."

After Melanie left, Shannon pointed herself toward the storeroom and the unfinished apple tart. *What I wouldn't give for twenty minutes to dash up the street to the diner for a quick meal.*

Essie set the phone down by the cash register as Shannon passed. "Matthew called from the park. He said you were going to loan him a couple easels for his booth to put signs on. He forgot to get them earlier."

Shannon did an about-face. The apple tart would have to wait. "I did say that."

"He's on his way here. He said he'd swing by the front of the store and grab them."

Shannon located two of the easels they used for display and headed toward the front door.

Matthew pulled up in his van, double-parking. He pushed open the driver's-side door and took the easels. After he shoved the easels in his van, Matthew gave Shannon a salute. "Thanks a million."

"You're welcome." She stood for a moment on the side-walk as he drove away. Traffic had thinned down a bit as folks gravitated toward places that served food. She crossed her arms over her chest, enjoying the coolness of the fall evening.

Across the street, the six thirty bus pulled up. Old man Caruthers disembarked carrying the single suitcase he took for his weekly visit to his daughter's house in Portland. His friend and pinochle partner, Jake Jenkins, greeted him at the curb. Jake slapped Caruthers's back like they hadn't seen each other in years and then directed him toward his car.

A sense of contentment spread through Shannon as she watched the scene unfold. When she'd inherited her grand-mother's house and moved to Apple Grove from Scotland, she didn't know if she would ever feel at home. But she did. Now she knew the locals and their habits. She'd discovered comfort could be found in watching Len Caruthers leave to visit his daughter every Monday and return on Tuesday, in hearing the string of school children race past her store window at three thirty every afternoon, and in talking to the regulars who showed up in her coffee bar at the same time each morning to socialize and work on their laptops. Apple Grove truly felt like home.

Shannon had just started to turn away when another passenger stepped off the bus—a tall woman with stiff posture. The woman clutched her purse close to her chest and glanced in one direction and then the other. No one came forward to greet her, and she appeared confused.

Shannon crossed the street and greeted the woman. "You look a little lost. Are you here for the Apple Festival?"

"Festival?" A perplexed look crossed the woman's face. Close up, Shannon estimated her to be in her mid-sixties. She was dressed in neutral colors, her salt-and-pepper hair pulled back into a bun. A look of weariness permeated the woman's demeanor, probably brought about by a long bus ride.

"So you're not here for the festival?" Shannon's curiosity piqued.

"Actually, I'm looking for a place called The Apple Grove

Inn." The woman walked toward her suitcase where the bus driver had left it and pulled out the retractable handle.

"That's up the street a couple of blocks. As a matter of fact, I'm heading that way soon to deliver some supplies to my friend. I'll walk you there if you can give me a minute to grab my things."

The woman tugged at her ear and glanced around nervously. "I don't want to cause you any inconvenience."

"It's no problem. My manager can close up the store. You're welcome to wait in the shop while I gather the supplies." The woman followed Shannon across the street, rolling her suitcase behind her, and stood at the front of the store in the wide archway that framed the entrance. Shannon grabbed the box of beads and then went to the storage room for the fabric samples, giving a forlorn glance to the apple tart, now looking less than appetizing after nearly half a day of sitting uncovered in the storage room.

Shannon bid Essie a good night and rejoined the woman. They exited the store and began walking down the sidewalk toward the inn. "I'm sorry, but I didn't catch your name."

The woman brushed back a wayward strand of hair that had come loose from her bun. "Helen. My name is Helen."

"And are you staying at the inn for the quilting workshops?"

"Actually, I'm here to see my sister. Perhaps you know her? Betty Russo. She owns the inn."

Shannon blinked. *I thought Betty told me her sister was dead!*

— 3 —

Stunned, Shannon felt her jaw sag as she stared at Helen. *Betty had said her only sister was dead, hadn't she?*

Shannon offered the reserved older woman a hesitant smile as she fought to regain her composure. "Well, welcome to Apple Grove. You picked a lively evening to arrive."

Helen nodded.

They walked in silence for a few minutes as Shannon struggled to find a conversation starter for the mysterious woman. The only sounds that broke the silence were their feet tapping the sidewalk and Helen's suitcase wheels rolling along the concrete. As they walked, they passed closed offices and shops. Most of Apple Grove shut down around suppertime, although the restaurants were bursting with activity.

As they turned the corner onto Meadowlark Street, she saw the black tile roof of the inn and the pale yellow exterior. Shannon didn't have much time to spare, but she really wanted to know how a dead sister could show up for a visit. *Best to prime the pump with safe questions.* "How was your trip? Do you enjoy riding the bus?"

"The trip was fine. My car isn't very reliable." Helen stopped for a moment to adjust her scarf against the fall chill. "The bus is easier, and I get around the city fine on public transport."

"Oh, so you live in Portland?"

"Yes."

Helen certainly didn't volunteer much information. They made their way up the driveway leading to the side of the inn where Betty and Tom lived, the same part of the inn containing the ransacked office. Though Tom and Betty had built additions over the years which made the inn appear unusually long, the main structure was originally a captain's mansion constructed in a Queen Anne Victorian-era style.

"I'll bet Betty will be surprised to see you," Shannon said, trying to squelch her unease. *Really surprised.*

Helen stopped abruptly. A strange expression flashed across her face—maybe fear, maybe sadness.

As quickly as the emotion rose to the surface, Helen covered it with a nervous smile. "We'll see."

Shannon tapped on the door and glanced at Helen. Her mouth formed a hard line. She was gripping the handle of the suitcase so tightly, her knuckles had turned white.

Betty opened the door. Her gaze fell first on Shannon and then on Helen. Nothing in her expression suggested that she recognized her sister.

Helen cleared her throat. "Hello, Eliza. I know … it's been awhile."

Betty opened her mouth to speak but only managed to shake her head in disbelief. Finally, when she did find her words, she whispered, "Helen?" Betty reached out to touch her sister with one finger as though she might be seeing a ghost.

Helen lifted her chin and stood a little straighter. "Yes, it's me."

"But I thought … we all assumed … oh my." Betty patted

her chest and spoke as though she'd run a mile. "Helen. *You* sent those quilts? Your quilts."

"I didn't have room on the bus to carry them. I meant for the package to arrive the same time I did," Helen said. "I wanted you to have them … as my coming-back-into-your-life gift."

Tears formed in Betty's eyes as she drew her sister into a stiff hug. "Why don't you come in?"

"Um, I'll leave these supplies here and leave you two to catch up." Shannon held the fabric out to Betty.

Betty clutched Shannon's arm. "No. Why don't you stay for a little bit?"

Shannon sensed desperation in Betty's touch. *Just what is the history between these two?*

As the three of them entered the inn's private residence, Tom's voice boomed from the next room. "Who was that?"

They stood in the little living room which featured numerous antiques. "It's Shannon and …" Betty hesitated. "… a visitor."

Tom appeared in the doorway, wiping his hands on a kitchen towel. He looked at Shannon and then at Helen.

Betty cleared her throat. "Tom, this is my sister, Helen."

Clearly confused by the statement, Tom's eyebrows shot up. "Uh-huh."

"Of course, you'll stay with us while you're in Apple Grove, won't you, Helen?" Betty's attempt at hospitality fell flat. The strain in her voice gave away how uncomfortable she felt.

"That would be nice." Helen tapped the suitcase handle nervously. "I guess there's some sort of Apple Festival going on in town, probably not a room to spare for fifty miles."

Betty bustled around the living room wiping unseen dust off an antique table. "I'm afraid all the larger rooms are reserved for guests who are coming for the quilting workshop. But we have an overflow room where we can set up an air mattress for you. The guests will be gone after the festival. I can move you into one of the nicer rooms then. I assume you're going to stay in town for at least a while." Betty said all the right things, but her words rang hollow.

"I'd like that," Helen said. Though she appeared to be well into her sixties, Helen revealed a little-girl vulnerability as she held her hands, fingers interlaced, in front of her stomach and lowered her head. "I know we have a lot of catching up to do."

Tom stepped forward. "Why don't I get Helen settled?"

"Thank you, honey." Husband and wife locked gazes in a moment of silent communication that only they understood. "I can set up a snack for us on the patio."

Tom grabbed Helen's suitcase. "If you'll come with me, the room is on the other side of the inn."

With a quick glance toward her sister, Helen followed Tom out of the room.

As soon as the door closed, Betty let out a heavy sigh.

Shannon allowed for the silence and waited for Betty to explain what in the world was going on.

Betty lifted her head and squared her shoulders. "I guess I better get that snack together."

Baffled, Shannon watched the older woman zip into the kitchen. "I'll help." The private residence which connected with the inn probably measured less than 800 square feet.

The small kitchen featured beige granite countertops and dark wood cabinets.

Shannon refrained from asking questions as Betty pulled out cheese, crackers, and cold cuts. Without a word, she handed Shannon a knife and cheese to slice, and then she shifted to the center island and sliced the summer sausage. The knife swung high and hit the cutting board repeatedly as Betty cut the meat with fervor.

"Betty?"

Betty didn't answer. Muttering to herself, she dug through the cupboards for a serving platter. As she arranged the crackers, her hands trembled.

Shannon touched her friend's arm and spoke tenderly, "You're in a state of shock."

Betty leaned against the countertop. "It's been nearly forty-five years." Her voice faltered.

Shannon set her knife on the cutting board. "More than forty years since you've seen your sister?"

Betty clutched her shirt collar at the neck. "I was only eight years old when she disappeared."

"She must be quite a bit older than you."

Betty got a faraway look in her eyes as though her memories played out before her on an invisible screen. "She's eleven years older. As a younger sister, I thought she hung the moon. I wanted to be like Helen."

"You loved your sister, but something must have happened. Why did you think she was dead?"

Betty's expression darkened. The furrow between her eyebrows intensified. "She started dating this older man. I don't know the whole story. I was so young. I remember hearing my parents having a heated discussion. The man had a criminal record. Mom and Dad didn't want Helen to be involved with him. And then one day, Helen disappeared, and my parents never said any more about it. Back then, families didn't discuss painful things." Betty pulled another tray from a shelf and placed four glasses on it. She gripped one of the glasses and looked out a window. "I never saw my sister again ... never knew what had happened to her. I thought she must be dead. Why else wouldn't she at least contact *me*?"

Shannon touched her friend's arm as tears formed in Betty's eyes. "That must've been so hard for you."

"Later I learned that my mother and father had given Helen an ultimatum—to choose between the family or the man. She chose." A tear trailed down her cheek. She swiped it away. "I don't know what to think. I don't even know how I feel right now. For forty-five years, she's been dead to me."

Shannon's throat grew tight over the pain and confusion her friend suffered. "This is a lot to deal with at once."

The sound of Helen and Tom's jovial conversation grew louder.

"Would you please stay?" Betty said. "I don't know what to say to her."

Shannon patted her friend's shoulder. "Sure."

Betty called out through the open door of the kitchen that connected to the rest of the inn. "If you two want to join us, we're headed outside to the patio."

Shannon grabbed the tray of snacks while Betty retrieved a pitcher of iced tea from the refrigerator.

Tom and Helen stood waiting for them when they

stepped through the kitchen door out onto the stone patio. Crisp cool air permeated the autumn evening. The sky transitioned from light blue to gray. The dry leaves, still hanging on some of the trees, rattled in the wind. Outdoor lighting washed the patio in warmth.

Tom tilted his head toward Helen. "It seems your sister likes classic cars as much as I do."

Leave it to Tom to find something in common with a woman who was a virtual stranger. Tom built bridges with almost everyone he met. It was one of the reasons owning the inn suited him so well. He genuinely loved people.

"I used to own a 1965 Mustang. Wish I hadn't sold that car." Helen turned to face her sister. "Eliza, do you remember that old Pontiac our parents owned?"

"I was so young, Helen. I really don't." Betty focused on removing food from the tray, her movements jerky.

"Most people call her Betty these days." Tom leaned toward Helen, his words holding no judgment.

"Oh, I'm so sorry. I didn't realize. We called you Eliza when you were little." Helen settled in a patio chair.

Though her friend did a good job of hiding her feelings, Shannon could imagine the emotions coursing through Betty, from sadness to joy to anger. She'd felt the same things when her mother, Beth Jacobs, resumed contact with her after more than thirty-five years.

From the age of four, Shannon's father had raised her alone in Scotland. Though Beth appeared to have abandoned her young daughter, the truth was she'd left without explanation to protect Shannon and her father. As a journalist, Beth worked to uncover information about a

European Mafia. When the Mafia threatened her life and the lives of her family, Beth went into hiding in the United States to protect herself and her family. Beth had revealed herself only after Shannon moved to Apple Grove to claim her inheritance. After an initial period of adjustment, Shannon now felt grateful for the opportunity to reconnect with her mother.

The conversation on the patio continued as late afternoon turned to dusk. Most of the talk centered on the upcoming festival and weather and preparation for the workshops at the inn. Though she shared things about their childhood, Helen gave away very little information about what had happened to her once she left home and cut off all communication with the family. If Helen had dated a man with a criminal record all those years ago, she may have gotten into trouble herself.

Shannon studied Helen as she spoke. Though her curious nature made it hard not to press for answers, she understood that the topic might be too raw for both sisters. She needed to trust, for her friend's sake, that everything would unfold in time.

Sunset made the fall evening grow cold, and Shannon tried to ignore the feeling that something more sinister lurked beneath the surface of Helen's arrival. She tamped down her suspicions, hoping the secrets Helen kept about her long absence wouldn't somehow end up hurting Betty.

— 4 —

Shannon awoke a little after dawn on Wednesday morning and shared a hurried hot beverage with Deborah, who intended to go to the inn and finalize the structure of the workshops with Betty. Deborah's remarkable quilting skills made her the best person to teach most of Betty's classes along with several other quilters in town.

As she stood at the counter sipping English breakfast tea, Shannon shared a bit about Helen's arrival. "I think Betty's still trying to sort through everything." Shannon wrapped her hands around the warm mug.

Deborah nodded wisely. Tall and regal, Deborah exuded a dignified manner. A jeweled barrette in her wavy white hair only added to the impression of royalty. "Family members can bring us the greatest joy, and they can also cause us the deepest wounds. I'll tread lightly around Betty. If she wants to share, she'll share."

Deborah's words echoed in Shannon's head as she climbed in her truck, the 1955 Ford she had inherited and had dubbed "Old Blue," and drove down the winding hill toward town. Her cellphone rang. She pulled over onto the shoulder to answer it without looking at the name and number on the screen.

"Hello." She pressed the phone against her ear.

"Shannon, it's Beth." Her mother's cheery voice echoed across the line.

"Good morning. How are things with you?"

"I meant to call you earlier. I made plans to drive one of my food trucks down to Apple Grove for the festival. Will you have time to visit?"

"I really hope so. But I have to warn you, I'm going to be very busy. Please don't be offended if I can't visit for long."

"I understand. I should be on the road in the next couple of hours, so I'll get there before lunchtime." Beth lived in Portland and owned several food trucks under the business name Gourmet on the Go.

Shannon said goodbye and clicked off the phone. In many ways, she was only a step or two further down the road than Betty in knowing how to deal with a loved one who'd popped back into her life after a long absence. But she wouldn't give up the second chance at a relationship with her mother for anything.

Shannon stared out at the beautiful fall morning, watching the signs of a town coming to life. A school bus whizzed by. Further down the road she could see Hattie Blaine raising the flag at the post office. The warmth of the early morning sun came through her windshield as she shifted her truck out of neutral.

Ten minutes later, Shannon parked in front of the darkened craft market. She used the hour before the shop officially opened to load up her fold-out booth for the festival. A local carpenter had designed it so that one person could set up the booth—and tear it down—with relative ease. After loading it, she grabbed a few other supplies and the sign that read "All proceeds go to fund cancer research" and jumped into her truck.

The park sat on the edge of town, south of the town square where some of the festival activities would take place. Booths in various states of completion filled the park. Shannon parked Old Blue and searched for her designated spot.

Kristin waved at her from across the park, her golden blond hair shining in the early morning sun.

What a welcome sight. Though she could have managed on her own, help made everything go faster.

Kristin ran over to greet her. "I don't live very far from here, so I thought I'd give you a hand before I head out for school."

"That would be great." She loved the way Kristin seemed to know what needed to be done without being told.

As Shannon unloaded the booth from the back of her old Ford, seeing such a high level of activity in the area so early in the morning surprised her. Roadies were already busy constructing the stage where several well-known singers and bands would perform on the final night of the festival, including the headliner, Angel Lewis. Some of the other crafters were putting the final touches on their booths in preparation for the festival, which would kick off in a few hours. Shannon walked past the huge banner that said "Crafts in the Park" to where Kristin had staked out their assigned spot.

The term "crafts" was used very loosely for the festival. Some of the booths featured face painting and massages. The festival provided a chance for local services and organizations to advertise as well as make money. Some booths featured hot dogs and slices of pizza for sale. Days ago, Joyce mentioned the Pink Sprinkles Bakery intended to sell baked goods, though Shannon didn't see the bakery cart yet. Beth's

Gourmet on the Go truck would fit right in when it arrived. Shannon suspected her mother had used driving the truck down as the excuse for them to spend time together—and she was touched.

Kristin worked at setting up the booth while Shannon pulled out signs and a plastic tub full of knitted hats and gloves from the bed of the truck. She hung some of the items for sale on the lattice part of the booth wall where a series of hooks allowed for display.

Kristin artfully arranged the merchandise with very little instruction.

"You've got a natural gift for display," Shannon said.

Kristin rocked on her feet, toe to heel, and smiled. "Thanks."

"I think Melanie said she would man the booth today, and then tonight we're going to get together to figure out a schedule, so someone will always be here." With everyone being so busy, Shannon wasn't sure how they would make that happen.

"I can pick up the slack if you need me to. I don't have school tomorrow," Kristin offered. "They gave us two days off because of the festival."

Shannon wrapped an arm around Kristin's shoulder. "I hoped you'd say that."

Shannon set up displays for her jewelry. She'd recently learned how to work with silver, which took her designs to a whole new level.

"Look, the doughnut cart arrived." Kristin pointed to the Pink Sprinkles Bakery cart being pulled by one of Joyce's employees on a motorcycle. "Would you like one?"

"That sounds delightful. I'm famished." A doughnut would hardly fill her up, but at least her belly wouldn't be empty. She made a mental note to get back on a sensible diet once the festival was over—lest she should have to buy all new pants.

While Kristin stepped into line with the other people waiting to start their day with a sugar buzz, Shannon arranged a sterling silver necklace on the neck model.

A girl in a cheerleading uniform sashayed over from a bake-sale table.

Shannon greeted the teenager as she examined the jewelry.

"These are pretty." The girl fingered a set of earrings made with royal blue glass beads.

"I can't start selling them until the official opening time. But I'll set it aside for you if you like. You probably have to get to school soon."

The girl shrugged. "I'll be here most of the day. We have permission to be out of school." She pointed back to the bake-sale table where several other cheerleaders sat. "We're trying to raise money so we can go with the football team to state. The school doesn't have the funds in the budget for us to go."

"I'm sorry to hear that. Good luck with your fundraising."

The girl looked at a pendant and then picked up a pair of earrings on a card. "I noticed Kristin O'Connor is working for you."

"Yes, she's a real delight." Shannon wondered if the teen might be fishing for a job. "For now, I only need her help during the festival and then maybe some on weekends. We'll see."

"She and her mom recently moved here from Texas." The teenager brushed her fingers through her hair, revealing rich red and blond streaks in it.

"I didn't realize they were new to town. I'm pretty new myself." Shannon put down the knitted cap she'd fidgeted with and looked directly at the girl. Now she suspected the girl's motive in coming over to the booth had nothing to do with previewing the jewelry for sale.

The girl leaned across the counter, glanced from side to side, and then whispered "Look, I think you better be careful. Kristin volunteered at one of our fundraisers, and some money disappeared."

"Really?"

"We couldn't prove anything, but I counted the money right before she took over for me. I'm pretty sure she put some in her pocket."

Shannon's defenses went up. "I haven't noticed anything like that. She's a wonderful worker."

The girl rolled her eyes. "I'm just telling you what I know."

Across the lawn, Kristin approached the booth, holding a cardboard tray containing doughnuts and coffee.

"I have to go." The girl pivoted, her cheerleader skirt flouncing from her swift turn.

Kristin handed Shannon a steaming cup of coffee from the tray. "I know that girl. I helped with their fundraiser. Mom said that to make friends, I should get involved with school activities. But those girls are kind of cliquish." Kristin lifted a doughnut off the tray. "What did she say to you?"

Shannon picked up on some nervousness in Kristin's question. "Nothing. She looked at the jewelry we have for sale."

Shannon glanced at the cheerleader as she took her seat at the bake-sale table. Nothing about Kristin suggested she was anything but an honest, hard worker. And yet the cheerleader had managed to plant seeds of doubt in Shannon's mind. The accusations caused old fears to rise to the surface. When she'd first arrived in Apple Grove, she'd caught the former manager of the Paisley Craft Market, Morgan Lombardi, embezzling from the store.

Shannon took a bite of doughnut. Icing coated her tongue, and she closed her eyes and sighed. Nobody else could do doughnuts like Joyce. "Pure heaven."

"I hope you like jelly-filled," Kristin said.

Shannon's mouth watered from the overload of sweetness. "Anything from Pink Sprinkles tastes great."

Kristin took several bites of her doughnut and then checked her watch. "I have to run to school. I'll come to the shop as soon as I'm done for the day."

"Great," Shannon said between bites.

Still munching on her doughnut, Kristin picked up her backpack and headed up the street to the high school. Shannon watched her, unable to let go of the doubt about Kristin. With great effort, she dismissed the bad thoughts and under her breath said, "See what gossip does?"

She finished arranging the rest of her inventory, sipped her coffee, and waited for Melanie to show up. The park quickly filled up with booths and vendors while the roadies worked on the stage. There was still no sign of Beth.

"You do beautiful work."

The voice jarred Shannon out of her worry over her mother.

A twenty-something woman with shiny black hair held one of Shannon's necklaces in her hand. Thick, long lashes framed the woman's bright blue eyes. It took Shannon a minute to place her. "You're umm ... that singer."

Color rose up in the woman's cheeks as her shoulders jerked up to her ears. "That's me."

The name finally popped into Shannon's head. "Angel Lewis." Shannon looked around for signs of a bodyguard or at least an entourage. "Are you here all by yourself?"

"Having lots of people around me all the time gets to be a bit much. Sometimes I need to escape." The singer's eyes twinkled with mischief. She wore neutral colors, but her distinctive dark hair stood out.

"But you must have some kind of security ...?"

"My manager contracted with Stone & McCrary for my public appearances. I don't think we need to worry about it though." Angel held one of the necklaces up to the morning light, allowing the pendant to twirl. "I remember Apple Grove as a pretty safe town."

"That depends on who you ask," Shannon said.

Angel leaned over the counter as though sharing a confidence. "If I dress down, people don't even know it's me."

"Really."

"Pull the makeup and fake eyelashes off. Slap on a hat." Angel grinned. "I can go down to the local grocery store without anyone knowing."

Shannon laughed. "I suppose if people aren't expecting to see you, they don't."

Angel still held the silver necklace in her hand.

"You like that necklace?"

"Yes, it's beautiful and unique." Angel lifted her gaze to study the knitted items displayed above her. "Everything here is so pretty."

"Do you knit?"

"No. Wish I could. No time to learn fun stuff like that with my concert schedule. I like making things, being creative. Lately, I've been sewing decorative pillows with silk fabric to give to my friends."

"You should visit my shop, the Paisley Craft Market on Main Street." Shannon pointed in the general direction of the store. "We have a nice selection of fabrics."

"Oh, that sounds like fun," Angel said. "Maybe, if I have time."

A tall, thin man with long hair pulled back in a ponytail approached Angel. He stopped a few booths away, crossed his arms and stared at her.

Shannon tilted her head. "That man acts like he knows you."

"He's my guitarist. We need to work out some melodies." Angel strutted over to the man, glanced over her shoulder, and waved at Shannon. "Catch you later."

"So much for my brush with fame," Shannon said to herself as she arranged the hand-painted scarves the Purls had created. She saw Melanie cutting through the playground.

Melanie waved to her from some distance away.

Smiling, Shannon waved back. Melanie's positive attitude lit up her whole face. The cancer survivor seemed to bring sunshine with her wherever she went. Melanie joined Shannon and gave the booth the once-over. "Looks like you've about got everything set up."

"And with time to spare." Shannon retreated to her truck and returned with a cash box, which she handed to Melanie.

Melanie took the box and said, "If the crowds in town are any indication, we should have some great sales this week." She stepped behind the counter. "I dropped off some flowers today at the inn." She tapped the counter with her fingers and bit her lower lip.

"And?"

"I met Helen. Betty told me how over forty years have gone by since they'd seen each other. How she thought her sister died years ago."

Shannon sipped her coffee. "It's a lot for Betty to deal with."

"I guess all we can do is be there for her," Melanie said, "and listen when she needs to talk."

"That's all any friend can do." Shannon glanced toward the stage as a van pulled up. Michael and several other men jumped out. She watched as the men circled the stage, inspecting wires and the lighting structure.

Melanie looked over at the stage area. "Getting ready for the concert, it looks like."

"Michael's firm is handling the security. I know this because I actually met Angel Lewis a few minutes before you showed up."

"No way!" Melanie looked at her with envy. "And I missed her by a few measly minutes."

"She's a really sweet girl," Shannon said as she watched Michael, who held a clipboard and spoke to one of the roadies.

Melanie followed the line of Shannon's gaze. "It wouldn't hurt to run over and say hello to him."

"He's busy. Besides, every time I talk to Michael, I end up feeling ... confused. After our first date fiasco ..."

Melanie leaned a little closer to her friend. "So what? Who doesn't have a first-date fiasco now and again? Your face still lights up whenever you see him."

Suddenly feeling self-conscious, Shannon touched her cheek. "It does?"

Melanie nodded for several seconds. "Go over and say hi. That's what *friends* do."

Shannon shrugged. "I suppose you're right." She traversed the browning lawn beneath trees that donned gold and red leaves.

Michael turned and locked eyes with her, and Shannon willed herself not to let her emotions get the best of her and force her to turn and run.

5

Michael saw Shannon approaching and strode toward her. "I thought I recognized you over there." His welcoming expression, the warmth in his voice, all of it confirmed that she shouldn't have worried about initiating a conversation with him.

Shannon felt her nervousness subside. "I hear you're doing security for the concert."

"I volunteered my team ... as a way of giving back to the community. We're also doing a paid job for the grand marshal of the parade, a singer named Angel Lewis."

"Oh yes, Angel. Believe it or not, I met her earlier. So she'll be in the parade *and* perform as the headliner?"

"And she'll attend a book signing downtown." Michael continued to watch the activity around the stage. "I think the chance to promote her new book clinched the deal."

"Angel can't be more than twenty-five years old. I'm not sure what someone that young would have to write about."

"It has lots of pictures," Michael said.

They both laughed.

"I've got a few other corporate jobs going as well. I'm stretched a little thin right now, so I hired extra help." Michael signaled to a blond man who was talking to a roadie. "Hey Dylan, come here a minute."

"Is there a problem, Mr. Stone?"

"No. I want to introduce you to someone. Dylan Manion, this is my friend Shannon McClain. She witnessed the break-in I told you about."

Dylan held out his hand to Shannon. "Nice to meet you."

Dressed in a pastel blue polo shirt and jeans, Dylan looked more like a college student than a security specialist. His nose angled to one side. He looked at her with a clear, intense gaze.

One of the other men gestured that something required Michael's attention.

"I guess I'd better let you get back to work," Shannon said.

"Unfortunately, duty calls," Michael said. "Good talking to you."

The two men strode back to the stage. Michael placed a hand on Dylan's shoulder, much like a father would do with a son. A twinge of sorrow rose to the surface as she watched. Ten years ago, a murderer had snatched away from Michael the likelihood of children when he had killed Michael's wife in a senseless act of revenge.

Shannon returned to the booth. After making sure Melanie didn't need anything, she climbed into Old Blue and drove to the craft market. She then spent the rest of the day in the shop helping Essie. As promised, Kristin showed up after school let out.

Shannon took off her apron and joined both of them near the register. "If you two think you can handle the store on your own, I'm going to head out. My mother was supposed to be here hours ago. I'm going to see if I can track her down.

I'm a little worried." She'd tried Beth's cellphone several times but got no answer. "And I have to pick up some food for the Purls meeting tonight."

"We can handle this," said Essie. "Can't we, Kristin?"

Kristin smiled. "I'm so happy I'm getting all these hours."

"And I'm so happy we found you," Shannon said. "Essie, would you show Kristin how to close and total out the receipts?"

Essie placed a bolt of fabric back on the shelf. "No problem. You go home and have a nice visit."

Shannon swung by the park again, thinking Beth might have gone directly there and been so swamped with customers, she couldn't call. She parked Old Blue in a short-term parking spot on the side of the street and weaved through the growing crowd on foot. Though the park brimmed with activity, she saw no sign of her mother's distinctive Gourmet on the Go truck. As she scanned the area, movement at the edge of the park caught her attention. A tall woman in a drab gray coat nearly blended in with the barren trees. *Helen.* Shannon recognized the salt-and-pepper hair. Helen stared off in one direction and then the other as though searching for someone.

"Hey, Helen!" Shannon stalked toward the trees. "Helen!"

Helen checked her watch, glanced around nervously, and disappeared into the trees. *Weird.* Shannon had shouted loud enough for the whole park to hear, yet Helen hadn't given the slightest response. As much as she wanted to for Betty's sake, Shannon couldn't let go of the notion Helen's sudden arrival in Apple Grove would lead to trouble. The fact that Helen had just ignored her had only reinforced her suspicions.

Still trying to sort through her uneasiness, Shannon returned to Old Blue and headed to the grocery store. *After forty-five years of no contact, why would Helen shown up now?*

Shannon perused the aisles of the grocery store, mindlessly putting things in her cart. Her ringing phone jerked her from her musing.

"Oh, thank goodness, I got hold of you." Her mother's voice vibrated through the phone.

"Is everything OK?"

"It is now. I encountered engine trouble before I made it out of Portland, but I'm on my way now. I should be there within the hour."

The hope of having some quality visiting time with her mother seemed to be fading. "Are you headed straight to the park?"

"Actually, I smell like diesel fuel. That's what you get when you try to do your own repairs. No one is going to buy food from me if I smell like a refinery. I need to take a shower. I suppose everything in town is booked up."

"Don't be ridiculous. The Paisley mansion is your home too. Go straight there. Deborah will let you in. Stay as long as you want." Offering the invitation came naturally.

A silence permeated the line before Beth responded. "Thank you. I'll be there soon."

"I might be tied up with errands, but I'll see you there eventually."

"Thanks, honey. I'm looking forward to spending some time with you." Her mother's words were infused with warmth.

Shannon said goodbye and held her phone close to her chest. How fortunate they both were to find each other again after so many years.

After paying for the groceries and stopping at several other places, Shannon took the winding road that led to 2121 Larkspur Lane. The three-story stucco mansion soon came into view. The Mediterranean-style home Shannon had inherited from her grandmother featured a terra-cotta tile roof and turrets on the front two corners of the house. Beth's Gourmet on the Go truck sat in the circle drive. Shannon climbed out of her truck, grabbed her groceries, and headed inside with a spring in her step.

Deborah appeared in the foyer. "Your mom's sleeping—in the summer house. I thought it might be quieter for her there since I was running the vacuum."

Shannon gave a furtive glance toward the summer house. "Oh."

Deborah placed a hand on her hip. "The poor dear was exhausted. She stayed up half the night getting the truck ready, and then it wouldn't start. She worked on it herself. Your mother has always been very resourceful that way. But she ended up having to take it to the mechanic after all. She was ready to collapse when she showed up here."

Shannon frowned. "She said she experienced engine trouble, but I didn't realize the extent of it."

"She showered while I made her some warm milk with honey, and then she pulled out the Murphy bed and went straight to sleep."

"I guess I'll catch up with her later." Shannon couldn't hide her disappointment.

"She'll be rested and ready for a visit in no time, I'm sure," Deborah said as she wiped her hands on her apron.

"I need to throw together a snack tray," Shannon said as Deborah helped her carry the bags to the kitchen. "The rest of the Purls will be here shortly. We have to figure out how we'll cover the booth in the park and still get everything else done that we need to do this week."

Shannon did a double take when she saw the enormous pile of fabric and quilting supplies covering the breakfast table.

"How are you getting all of this over to the inn?" she asked, setting a bag of groceries on the rose granite countertop.

"Len Caruthers is coming by later with his truck. He's got two young men from the church to help him. They're going to transport my quilting frame too."

Shannon rummaged through the cupboards to find a serving tray. On impulse, she decided she would also bake orange-cranberry scones. If she timed it right, they'd be warm from the oven when the Purls arrived. She filled the kettle with water and pulled down a basket of assorted teas. Hot tea, warm scones with butter and jam, and a tray with crackers and cheeses—the perfect treat for a cool fall evening.

As she worked, she heard Len pull up in his truck and Deborah bark commands as they loaded the quilt frame into the back. The two teenage boys made repeated trips to the kitchen table, picking up the boxes Deborah had set out. Shannon couldn't imagine Deborah needing so many supplies. Most of the quilters would bring their own materials. Many had been in the shop to pick up fabric and batting already.

She popped the scones into the oven and heard Len's

truck sputter away down the road. A quiet settled in the house, and Shannon decided Deborah must have ridden along with Len to supervise the unloading as well.

Shannon opened a few new boxes of tea and arranged them in the basket. While she waited for the oven timer to go off for the scones, she stared out the window at the summer house, which still looked quiet. Nobody passed by the window, and the lights remained dimmed.

She'd really been looking forward to visiting with Beth. She wiped down counters, feeling a little disappointed; so much for having a plan.

The timer dinged at the same moment someone rang the front doorbell. "Be there in a second," Shannon called out. She quickly pulled the scones from the oven and ran to open the door. Kate and Betty stood waiting patiently on her front steps. "Come on in. I'm finishing up in the kitchen if you all want to get settled in the study."

"Joyce is helping Melanie load up the inventory," Kate explained. "They should be here any minute." As usual, Kate was dressed in jeans and an animal-themed T-shirt—fitting attire for the owner of Ultimutt Grooming.

In the kitchen, Shannon placed the scones in a basket lined with a piece of floral fabric and set the warm teapot on a tea tray.

Betty stepped into the kitchen. "Do you need help with anything?"

"I think I've got it under control," Shannon said, arranging the sugar bowl and cream pitcher. Sensing that Betty wanted to talk, she asked, "How are things going with Helen?"

"All right. We spent most of the day getting last-minute things together for the workshops, and then she needed to go for a walk alone. We really didn't have much time to visit."

Shannon dried her hands on a towel. Helen must have been on her "alone walk" when Shannon saw her in the park earlier. Again, Shannon fought off her rising suspicion over Helen. She didn't want to upset Betty over what might be nothing.

Betty lowered her voice as a tinge of irritation colored her words. "I wish she would have called ahead of time. Not only would it have given me time to prepare for the shock of seeing her after thinking her dead for all of these years, but this is the worst time for a visit because I'm so busy with the workshops." She threw her hands in the air. "And then this stupid break-in. It has me jumping at every little noise in the inn."

"Has Grayson called you? Did they find fingerprints or anything that might help?"

"He's no closer to an answer than he was yesterday." Betty picked a paper napkin off the tray and folded it mindlessly. "What if the thief comes back? What if he didn't find what he was looking for the first time?" Her voice cracked.

That fear festered in Shannon's mind as well. Maybe the thief *did* steal something, but then again, maybe not. Shannon had interrupted him. What if he came back to finish the job? She didn't want to feed Betty's anxiety by talking about the robbery.

"Yesterday was quite a day for you ... not just because of the break-in," Shannon said. With the memory of her own roller coaster of emotions toward her mother still crystal clear, Shannon had a feeling that she knew why Betty had come into the kitchen. "How are you feeling about Helen coming back into your life?"

Betty let out breath. She stood up straighter, as though a heavy weight no longer rested on her shoulders. "I don't understand myself sometimes. When those quilts arrived, I knew without a doubt that they were my sister's. I thought someone had finally gotten around to sending them to me per her last wish. It made me sad to think about how things could've been different if she'd never left home—how I would've had my sister in my life."

Shannon picked up the tea tray. "But then when she showed up …"

Betty touched her fingers to her temples and closed her eyes. "I don't know how to explain it. There's a part of me that was relieved, but then I started feeling angry that she was alive and had waited so long to get in touch."

Shannon set down the tray and drew her friend into an embrace. "I understand. Believe me, I understand. Do you have any idea why she chose to contact you now?"

Betty sighed. "No. And honestly, sometimes I get suspicious. Then I immediately feel guilty about it."

"Has she said something to make you doubt her intentions?"

"Not exactly. She's changed a lot from what I remember. She seems—" The doorbell rang for the second time. "Never mind. Let's forget it for now. I'll let the others in."

Within minutes, all five of the Purls sat in the study, spreading butter on their scones and sipping warm tea.

Shannon took out her day planner. "OK, first thing tomorrow, Joyce is going to serve treats at Betty's workshop, and I'll teach one of the opening classes."

"I can watch our booth for most of the morning," said Kate.

"Good." Shannon made a note on her planner. "Then later in the day, I can send Kristin, my high school helper, over. Or maybe I'll be able to do it myself."

With the schedule for manning the Purls' booth in the park completed, talk turned to other things going on at the festival.

Melanie raved about the Apple Queen float. "I can't wait for the parade tomorrow. But I am worried about one thing." She bit her lower lip and looked around the room. "I put a ton of those silk flowers on the Apple Queen's gown, and they are all scented with my special perfume. I hope it's not too over the top."

The group chimed in with their opinions. Every once in a while, Shannon noticed Betty get a faraway look in her eyes and then draw her attention back to the group, offering a smile that didn't quite reach her eyes.

Kate piped up, "So Betty, how are things going with your sister?"

The Apple Grove rumor mill was nothing if not efficient. By now the whole town had probably heard bits and pieces of Betty's story.

Betty sat up a little straighter and clutched her teacup tightly. "It's going as expected. We're taking it one day—well, one hour—at a time."

Melanie spoke slowly as though choosing her words carefully. "Has she said where she's been all these years?"

"Not exactly, no." Betty ran her finger around the rim of her teacup and then cast a furtive glance in Shannon's direction.

The other Purls would be sensitive around Betty. They were four of the kindest women Shannon knew. But Shannon could see that Betty felt uncomfortable talking about her sister with everyone. She changed the subject, and they all chatted about other things for a while longer.

The women said their good-nights at the door, and Shannon offered Betty an extra-long hug. She didn't have any great wisdom to give to her friend. Something about Helen's mysterious appearance wasn't right. Shannon knew it in her heart. Helen had over forty years to account for. If she had wanted a clean slate between her and Betty, she should be eager to give an explanation. *Why was she being so secretive about her past?*

Shannon didn't want to upset Betty by blurting out her suspicions. All she could share was the knowledge that she understood Betty's up-and-down feelings. She watched from the porch as Betty and Kate pulled through the circular driveway, the car taillights glowing like red monster eyes as they disappeared down the hill.

Completely exhausted, Shannon collapsed into an over-stuffed chair in the study. She leaned back and closed her eyes. *What a day.*

She picked up a mystery novel she'd been reading as headlights reflected on the windows. Deborah called out her goodbye to Len from the front steps. Then the older woman entered the house, peeking into the study to say good night before retiring to her bedroom.

Shannon returned her attention to her book, and the house grew silent. With only the ticking of the grandfather clock for noise, she lost herself in the story.

As she turned the page, she caught a brief flash of movement out of the corner of her eye and looked up. Immediately, she jerked to her feet, the book falling to the floor.

Someone is outside the window.

— 6 —

Shannon crept toward the window but saw no sign of a person. She'd only noticed the movement in her peripheral vision. *Maybe it was just a branch blowing in the wind.* She hurried to the kitchen and stepped outside, facing the lake.

Dark shadows fluttered among the trees in the distance. Deborah wasn't in the habit of taking late-night walks, and Beth surely would have knocked on the door once she had woken up.

Shannon stepped off the porch as her heart rate kicked into high gear. She saw another flash of movement—this time she got a better look. A human form had definitely zigzagged through the trees near the edge of the lake.

Betty's break-in reminded Shannon that a burglar might target the town during this busy time. Perhaps the Paisley mansion was next on the thief's list. Shannon turned and started back toward the house to call the police, but a laugh that sounded like birdsong halted her steps.

Most thieves don't giggle when they're trying to rob a house.

She stepped toward the trees and shouted, "Who's out there?"

"Shannon, is that you?" Her mother's voice had a soft, lilting quality.

"Beth? What are you doing out here?"

Beth broke away from the trees. Her red, wavy hair

caught the light spilling out from the house, taking on a shimmering quality. "I was on my way to knock on the door when I heard the fish jumping in the lake. This time of night in the fall is so wonderful. As a teenager going through the usual adolescent angst, I used to sit down by the lake until the world felt right again."

Shannon had to keep reminding herself that her mother had grown up in this very home. "You used to do that?"

"Come with me." Beth reached out and took Shannon's hand, leading her down the stone pathway to the lake. When they reached the edge, Beth gathered in her full skirt and settled down beside the water.

"What are some of the other things you remember about the house?" Shannon asked, always eager to learn more about her mother's childhood.

Beth made a shushing noise, tilted her head, and closed her eyes. "Listen."

Shannon could feel hurt rising to the surface. *Doesn't she want to talk?*

"Close your eyes," Beth encouraged, her voice filled with anticipation.

Shannon closed her eyes. Gradually, she heard the sounds of the fish feeding at the surface of the water, branches creaking in the wind, and waves lapping at the shore of the lake. As she listened more closely, she detected the muffled roar of the ocean in the distance and the faint scent of salt air. Though the ocean wasn't close, a person could see it from the upper stories of the mansion.

When Shannon opened her eyes, a three-quarter moon cast golden shadows across the water.

After at long while, Beth spoke up, "Wasn't that something?"

"That was quite a show." A sense of contentment flooded through Shannon. "I could sit here enjoying it all night."

"Except that you've got a big day ahead of you." Beth pressed her shoulder against Shannon's. "I suppose you need to get to bed."

Shannon let out a heavy sigh. "I suppose. Tomorrow is going to be busy."

"This day didn't go at all how I intended," Beth said. "I thought we'd get to see more of each other. But I'm sure we'll have some time this week in the evenings." The statement had almost come out as a question.

"I sure hope so. This festival is keeping me on my toes." Shannon found herself wishing that her mother had come at a less busy time.

Beth stood up, brushing the grass and dirt off her skirt. "I should try to get a few more hours of sleep too."

"Why don't you take one of the guest rooms in the house?" Shannon rose.

"That sounds like a great idea. Let me get my overnight bag out of the truck."

"I'll help you."

Shannon led Beth to a prepared guest room and retreated to her own bedroom. She fell into bed with a sense of satisfaction. *Life has a way of unfolding in wonderful and unexpected ways.* She'd seen a new side of her mother tonight. A glimpse into Beth's childhood had somehow helped Shannon understand her mother better, no conversation required.

Shannon rolled onto her side and drew the blankets up

to her shoulders. Tomorrow, she'd be running a hundred miles an hour the second her feet hit the ground. She was grateful her class was one of the first of Betty's workshops. Maybe afterward she would get a chance to speak with Helen alone and find out what she'd been doing for the last forty or so years while everyone presumed her dead.

She couldn't help but wonder if prison had been part of the picture. Even so, Betty deserved an explanation for her sister's long absence.

*   *   *

Thursday morning, when Shannon pulled up to The Apple Grove Inn, she had to search far and wide for a parking space. No surprise about that. All the guests for the workshops had arrived, as had many of the festival goers.

Shannon grabbed a box of last-minute supplies from the passenger seat and headed inside. As she passed through the tearoom, she nearly collided with Joyce, who burst out of the swinging kitchen door holding a three-tiered tray that featured an assortment of muffins.

"We've got quite a crowd," Joyce said, rebalancing the teetering tray. "I'm helping Gertrude with everything." Gertrude was Deborah's sister, who worked part time as the pastry chef and cook for the inn. She'd agreed to work more hours over the course of the festival to keep up with the demand.

"Oh good, I'm sure Betty will appreciate the extra help." Shannon hugged the box she carried and looked around the room. "There are more men here than I'd expected to see."

Joyce nodded. "Some of the husbands might sit in on the classes with their wives, but for those who choose not to, Tom has appointed himself the entertainment committee for 'quilting widowers.' So I think we have everything under control. Good luck with your class this morning." With a wink, Joyce headed toward the meeting room to replenish the snacks.

Less than fifteen minutes later, Shannon began her class on how to incorporate beading into quilt blocks. Every seat in the room was full, and the bright-eyed attendees gave her a hearty round of applause when she concluded her presentation. After answering a few questions, she excused herself.

Maybe now I can get Helen alone and talk to her. Shannon popped her head into the kitchen where Tom, Betty, and Gertrude worked frantically to prepare lunch.

Betty stood before a large cutting block that was surrounded by vegetables. She offered Shannon a warm smile. "How did the class go?"

"It was very well received, and there were lots of great questions."

"Good. We're trying to get this lunch pulled together." Betty picked up a carrot and chopped it.

"Where's Helen?"

Betty placed chopped tomatoes and carrots into a huge lettuce-filled bowl. "She said something about catching a nap." Betty's voice still sounded a little strained. "She helped out quite a bit this morning."

But probably didn't tell you anything about where she's been for the last forty-five years. Shannon had a feeling

Helen wasn't napping. "Things at the store are covered for now. I think I might hang out here a little longer."

She wandered around the lounge. Most of the students seemed engrossed in their projects or had returned to their rooms. She peeked into the tearoom where Livvy, the waitress, was busy arranging centerpieces of fresh flowers for the tables.

When Shannon looked out the window, she noticed a Stone & McCrary vehicle parked outside. She hadn't seen Michael around, but she figured he must have made good on his promise to check the security system. She searched the public areas of the inn, hoping she might run into him. Michael was the one person with whom she could safely share her suspicions about Helen. She spotted one of his employees outside, but no Michael.

The inn wasn't exactly Michael's usual high-dollar clientele. He'd probably only installed the security system because he felt some loyalty to the people of Apple Grove. Perhaps he'd only sent employees to make sure the inn was secure.

She stepped outside, nodding in the direction of the two Stone & McCrary Security staff members. She recognized the one who held a phone to his ear as Dylan Manion, the new employee she'd met the day before. The other worker, a middle-aged man with a receding hairline, stood studying the keypad by the back door.

"Did Michael come with you?" she asked Dylan.

Dylan angled the phone away from his head. "Yeah, he's around here somewhere."

She searched the backyard, reluctantly admitting to herself that she'd certainly used up a lot of time trying to "casually" run into him. Her neck muscles tensed with frustration. She shouldn't let Michael occupy so much space in her head. He'd made it clear by his recent actions he wanted to be nothing more than friends.

As she drew near to a grove of trees, the sound of a woman's frantic voice reached her ears and pulled her from her mulling.

"I don't know if this is such a good idea," the woman said. "Betty is not what I expected."

Shannon froze, and her ears perked up at the mention of her friend. She heard no reply to the woman's statement, only silence. *She must be talking on the phone.* Shannon slipped further behind a tree, realizing the voice was Helen's. She could only pick up bits and pieces of the conversation as it faded in and out due to Helen pacing as she talked.

"This is all too much for me. I don't know if I can make it work," Helen said.

Shannon stayed hidden until Helen emerged from the trees. She pressed her back against the trunk of a tree and watched Helen walk toward the inn, trying to digest what she'd just heard. *Have I been right about Helen all along? Her motives for returning may not be so innocent.*

Really, Helen could have simply been saying that it had been a bad idea to come back into her sister's life—that it was too much for her to deal with—some of the same feelings Betty had expressed. But whoever Helen was talking to had caused her tone to be defensive and even a little fearful.

As Shannon walked back toward the inn, she couldn't let go of the idea that something more was going on—something that could ultimately put her friend in danger of being hurt emotionally. Or worse.

Betty met Shannon as she stepped across the threshold. "Oh, there you are," Betty said, holding a large tray filled with salad plates.

"Did you need my help?" Shannon heard chatter and laughter spill out from the tearoom as the quilters and other guests settled in for their lunch.

"We've got lunch under control, but one of the guests has fallen ill. His wife is taking care of him, and I said I would take her up a sandwich. Everything is prepared already. It's sitting on a tray in the kitchen, if you wouldn't mind running it upstairs."

"I can do that, no problem," Shannon said.

"You're a lifesaver. Room 206."

"I just saw Helen a minute ago." Shannon chose her words carefully. "Has she opened up to you at all about why she stayed away so long?"

Betty shook her head. "Every time I bring it up, she wants to talk about when we were children." She stared off into the distance. "I have my sister back in my life. I don't want to push her away by demanding explanations."

Someone called Betty's name from the serving area.

"Go," Shannon said. "I'll take the sandwiches up to room 206."

She squeezed her way into the busy kitchen where waitresses rushed in and out. Helen stood beside the dishwasher unloading plates. She lifted her head in acknowledgement of Shannon.

"Keeping busy?" Shannon asked as she found the tray containing sandwiches, napkins, and two milk cartons.

"I want to help Betty any way I can." Helen handed a

plate to a waitress. Nothing in her demeanor indicated she had any awareness that Shannon had overheard her phone conversation.

"I'm sure you do," said Shannon. "It must have been tough, being cut off from family for all those years. But I'm sure you've made some close friends in ... Portland?"

Color rose up in Helen's cheeks as she delivered her terse words. "I keep mostly to myself." She turned away, arranging some glasses that were already tidy.

Ah ... so, I struck a nerve.

Holding the tray, Shannon pushed open the swinging doors of the kitchen. On her way upstairs, she grabbed some of Joyce's leftover treats and arranged them on a pretty napkin.

When she knocked on the door of room 206, a short woman with dark, curly hair answered the door.

"Oh, thank goodness. I'm starving, but I didn't want to leave Jeremy." She turned slightly sideways to reveal a lump underneath a blanket. "He's going to be OK; I don't think it's the flu or anything contagious. He gets such a restless stomach when we travel."

Shannon handed her the tray. "Glad to hear it wasn't anything he ate."

"Are you kidding? The food here is great." The woman removed the food and handed the tray back to Shannon. "I'm Jackie, by the way."

"Shannon McClain."

"Yes, of course, I'm sorry I missed your class today. I was able to make the first one, but then Jeremy called me on my cell. Said he didn't want to be alone. You know how men can be when they're sick—they turn into little boys again."

Shannon laughed even as she felt a stab of pain in her heart. Her husband, John, had been a true Scotsman, tough to the bone. He'd be on death's door before she heard so much as a whimper from him. She managed a smile. "Jackie, it was nice meeting you. I'm sure I'll see you and Jeremy around."

Jackie closed the door, and Shannon stood in the hallway for a moment. She hadn't thought of John in a while. Funny how grief could rise to the surface at the most unexpected times. Noises down the hall drew her attention.

When she walked past the supply closet, she saw Dylan Manion inside, leaning against one wall.

"Hi, Dylan. What are you doing up here?"

Dylan whirled around, a look of surprise coloring his features. "Dealing with some security issues." Though his expression remained composed, not giving away any clear emotion, she noticed a slight eye twitch.

Security issues in a supply closet? That's a new one.

"I didn't realize part of the security system was in there," said Shannon.

Dylan offered no explanation.

She pressed the tray against her chest. "Well, I'm headed back downstairs."

Dylan's gaze darted up and down the hall, indicating nervousness. "Did you ever catch up with Michael?"

"No."

"He's around here somewhere."

"I'm sure he is." Shannon studied Dylan for a moment longer before moving on.

The crowd in the tearoom had thinned a little. Helen

chatted with guests while Betty loaded dirty dishes into a tub. Helen was all smiles and laughter with the guests, quite a switch from when Shannon had pressed for details about her life in Portland. It made sense that both sisters would have feelings they needed to work through, but if Helen was planning on leaving because this was "all too much for her," shouldn't Betty be warned? Shannon felt a need to protect her friend's heart.

"I understand you're looking for me."

Shannon was startled. She hadn't heard Michael walk up behind her. "Och! You surprised me."

He grinned. "Sorry."

"I saw the company truck outside, and I thought you might be around. Did you figure out anything about the security system?"

"The system works fine. Like you said, it wasn't activated the day of the robbery. In fact, I think the Russos turn it off quite a bit. Apparently, guests accidently trigger the alarms, and they decided it would be less unpleasant to turn the system off."

Taking note of the time, Shannon strolled toward the front entrance, and Michael followed her lead. "That makes sense. They do have to keep their guests happy." They stepped outside, and Shannon turned to face him.

Michael placed his hands on his hips. "Keeping clients safe is important too."

She hadn't meant to offend him or tell him how to do his job. "Point taken. Betty's greatest concern is making sure her guests have a nice stay here. That's all I meant."

"It might make sense to put their private residence and

office on a separate system." His voice had taken on a passion she often picked up on when he talked about his job. "Having a system in place is useless if they don't turn the thing on."

Shannon knew Betty and Tom focused on the comfort of their guests. She let the issue go. She couldn't win an argument about security with Michael. If he had his way, every house and business would be cinched up tighter than Fort Knox. "By the way, I saw Dylan upstairs. He acted a little strange."

Michael's back stiffened defensively. "What do you mean?"

"He said there was a security issue ... in the supply closet."

Michael cocked an eyebrow. She could feel the wall go up between them. "He knows what he's doing."

She dared not say anything else. It seemed no matter what conversational path they went down lately, things turned sour. Shannon stood listening to the fall leaves rustle and stared at the conundrum in front of her—the riddle known as Michael Stone. She hadn't intended to get into a disagreement over the Russos' priorities for the inn or Dylan's weird behavior, and now she had lost all desire to talk to him about Helen.

"You take care, Michael." She touched his forearm, and he responded with a slight smile. "I've got to get back to the craft market before the parade starts and they block off the street."

7

From inside the Paisley Craft Market, Shannon could feel the excitement build as people lined the sidewalk to watch the parade. Once the high school marching band could be heard a couple of blocks away, all the customers vacated the store.

Shannon took off her work apron and spoke to Kristin and Essie. "Ladies, we are not going to make any sales until that parade goes by. We might as well step out and enjoy it."

The sidewalk overflowed with people, but Shannon managed to wedge her way between a father with his son perched on his shoulders and a group of three boys who looked to be about seven or eight years old.

Across the street on the roof of a two-story office building, Michael paced, holding his hand to his ear. His post from atop the building gave him a bird's-eye view of the parade and surrounding neighborhood. Shannon doubted that the parade's grand marshal, the young pop star Angel Lewis, was in any real danger in Apple Grove. Maybe she'd simply hired Michael's firm as her security detail because she needed to find a way to spend all the money she'd made since hitting the big time.

The intense rhythm and melody of the marching band grew louder as they drew near. The sound escalated and then faded as they passed by. They made their way up Main

Street, marching past the seemingly endless line of onlookers, trailing behind riders in floats advertising local businesses. Clowns threw out candy to the children who darted into the street and back again, collecting the booty. When Angel Lewis passed by, waving from the back of a pink convertible, her gaze went up to the Paisley Craft Market sign, and recognition flashed in her expression when she made eye contact with Shannon.

Melanie's float with the Apple Queen and her court soon rolled into view, and Shannon clapped and cheered. As the float passed by, Shannon noticed a distinct scent. At first she thought it was coming from the float. After all, Melanie had promised the first smell-o-rama float ever. But the scent wasn't floral. However, it *was* familiar.

It's the same scent I smelled the day the inn was robbed— the intruder's cologne!

Squeezed in on all sides by the crowd, Shannon tried to turn. "Excuse me." She pushed through the crowd, certain the smell had come downwind and from behind her.

An older couple parted so she could get by.

"Pardon me, I need to get through." As she worked her way toward the storefront, a dark-haired man met her gaze. His eyes grew wide, and then he turned and ran down the alley. Shannon pursued him. The noise of the cheering crowd and the parade dimmed as she sprinted along the side streets.

The rest of town was virtually deserted due to the parade. She bolted up the alley and turned onto a side street, searching everywhere. There was no sign of the man. Trying to catch her breath, Shannon jogged down the street, checking the alleys as she passed. Most of the stores were locked up. She peeked into a Laundromat and saw that the back door swung on its hinges.

Inside, washing machines chugged and dryers whirred, but only one lone elderly man sat with his legs crossed, reading a newspaper.

Shannon raced into the humid room. "Did a dark-haired man just come through here?"

The man put down his newspaper and adjusted his glasses on his bulbous nose. He spoke with a slow, measured tone. "Don't much care for parades."

"Did a dark-haired man come through here?" After repeating her question more loudly, Shannon walked to the open back door and glanced up and down the side street, seeing nothing. "Is this door open all the time?"

The old man lifted his head. "It's the crowds I don't like. I've never much cared for lots of people packed into a tight space. Makes me feel like a sardine." The man held up the newspaper again, hiding his face. "He came through here a second before you showed up hollering questions. Most action I've seen all day."

Shannon ran out the back door. She jogged past several buildings, fearing she had lost too much time. He could be five blocks away by now, or he might have hopped into a car and driven away.

A young mother with a child in a stroller stopped by a car and opened the back door. She was lifting her child out of the stroller as Shannon jogged by. "Are you chasing that crazy dark-haired guy running through town?" she asked.

"Yes." Shannon's hopes rose. "You saw him?"

"He nearly knocked me over; he ran that way." The woman pointed up the street. "He took a right at the yellow house. He acted like somebody was after him, looking over his shoulder and stuff."

Shannon thanked her and raced toward the yellow house. She turned into an alley lined with multistory buildings with fire escapes running down the sides. Heavy footsteps echoed against metal stairs as the elusive man bolted up a fire escape. Shannon sprinted toward the ladder at the bottom of the fire escape.

"Stop! I want to talk to you," she shouted, nearly out of breath from running.

The man kept climbing.

Shannon gained on him, coming within a few yards of the man as she climbed up the fire escape ladder that led to a platform where the stairs began. The man turned suddenly and raced back down a few steps. She saw his face clearly for only a second, and then her vision filled with the underside of a boot.

Shannon felt herself falling through space toward the hard concrete. She braced for a painful collision, but instead, strong arms caught her, breaking her fall.

Still stunned from the blow to her head, she blinked. "Michael?"

"I saw you leave the parade. I have men stationed all over the place on rooftops. They told me which way you ran."

Shannon stared up at the building, her vision clearing. The thief was nowhere to be seen. He'd probably found an escape route on the other side. "He got away ... again."

"Maybe not," said Michael. He carefully lowered Shannon

so she could stand, and with one arm still wrapped around her, he spoke into the microphone on his other wrist. "Team four; be on the lookout for a dark-haired man in a white shirt. Subject is not a threat to our client, but is a person of interest." He offered her a soft smile that brought light to his blue eyes. "We might still catch him."

Still a little dazed, she said, "I can't believe that just happened. You caught me. Like something out of a ridiculous fairy tale. Sometimes I think ... you must be my knight in shining armor." She blinked rapidly a few times to clear her vision.

Michael continued to keep Shannon in the circle of his arm, so close that she could breathe in his soapy cleanness. The magnetic power of his gaze drew her in. It wasn't the blow to the head from the thief's boot that was making her dizzy anymore. "I think I can stand on my own."

"You're sure?" Michael released his hold on her waist and edged away. The warmth of his arm against her body faded slowly.

She took a deep breath. "Yes."

"Who was that guy anyway?"

"I'm pretty sure he's the man who tried to rob Betty the other day. His cologne was really memorable." She touched her head where a bump had already formed.

Michael drew his eyebrows together. "I doubt if it's a one-of-a-kind cologne."

Shannon felt her defenses go up, chasing away the last bit of fog in her brain. "He ran when he saw me coming toward him. He recognized me. Only a guilty man would do that."

Michael nodded slowly. "OK ... that's pretty good evidence

that he was up to something." He stepped closer to her, his expression growing serious. He touched her forehead. "You're going to have quite a bump." His touch felt as soft as butterfly wings brushing over her skin. "Perhaps we should go to the ER and let them take a look."

Shannon sighed. "That's not necessary. I'll be OK."

Michael drew back his hand and thought for a moment. "So you got a look at the guy this time?"

She nodded. The man's face was burned into her memory. "Yes, I have more than cologne to go on now."

"If my team doesn't spot him, maybe we should go talk to Grayson ... see if we can get an ID on the guy."

"That's a good idea."

The noise of the parade faded out completely. A slow stream of people began to fill the side streets. Shops opened up, and people returned to their cars.

"Why don't we go to my office and wait for my security teams to check in?" Michael escorted Shannon the short distance to his office, which was located on the town square, on Ocean Avenue. Once there, he offered her an ice pack for her head. After the parade ended, the team still watching Angel Lewis radioed in that she was safely on her way to Portland.

Shannon wandered around the small office that had no true reception area, only a room with lots of file cabinets, boxes of files, and several computers. It wasn't the office Michael usually used to meet clients; that office was located in Portland.

In the clutter of the room, a stack of books caught her eye. The cover featured Angel Lewis with her long false eyelashes, dark hair, and eyes so intensely blue that the color had to have come from contact lenses or been re-touched. Her smile was genuine though. She had a capti-vating presence, even in a photograph. Shannon read the title, *My Life in the Whirlwind*, a reference to her hit song and first album, both of which were titled *Whirlwind*.

"You can have one of those books if you want." Michael swung around in his office chair. "She gave us a bunch of free copies."

Shannon lifted the book and hugged it close. "Thanks. I'll take one."

Team four radioed in that they'd been unable to find the dark-haired man.

"Come on, I'll drive you to the police station," Michael offered.

Shannon could feel a headache coming on as she slid into the passenger seat of Michael's Lexus. The man had kicked her pretty hard. While Michael drove, she tried to recall the details of the man's face. *Dark, curly hair and a mustache, in his thirties or forties ...*

She pulled the ice pack off her forehead and lifted the hair that covered the red welt.

Michael glanced over at her and winced. "Will I ever be able to convince you to leave the investigating to the police and us professionals?"

Again, Shannon could feel her hackles going up. "There wasn't a policeman in sight. They were all occupied with the parade. I think I handled it OK. I got a good look at the man at least."

He held up a hand toward her as though to stop the

force of her words. "You handled it fine, but I don't want to see you hurt. What if he'd used a gun instead of a heavy boot?"

Grayson pulled into the parking lot of the police station at the same time they did. He climbed out of his SUV and strode toward them. "That was some parade, huh?"

Shannon didn't feel the need for small talk. "Chief, I think I may have seen the man who broke into the inn the other day."

The smile faded from Grayson's face. "Come on inside, and I'll take down the information. All the other officers are still out dealing with traffic headaches from the parade." He held the door open for Shannon. "It's kind of quiet in here."

Shannon stepped into the station with Michael following close behind her.

Grayson lowered himself into his office chair and positioned his fingers on the computer keyboard. "So what can you tell me about the alleged perpetrator?"

Shannon pieced together details as they came back to her while the chief typed. After she finished, Grayson suggested she look through a database of known criminals in the area to see if any of them looked familiar. After accessing the database, Grayson offered her his chair and moved away from his desk to allow her to concentrate. Shannon focused on the monitor and clicked through the photographs.

Michael brought her a cup of coffee and then also left her alone.

As she looked through the pictures, she could hear Michael and Grayson talking and laughing. Having been a police officer himself, Michael seemed to have a natural camaraderie with the chief, which was more than she could say about her relationship with Grayson. Not that they were enemies. He did his job well, and she respected him for that. But where crime was concerned, her curiosity often got the better of her, and Grayson didn't like that.

One criminal after another flashed across the screen. Though they spoke in low tones, Shannon caught bits and pieces of Grayson and Michael's conversation as she focused on each mug shot. Michael said something about it all being in the timing, and Grayson chuckled.

Shannon sat up a little straighter in her chair. *All in the timing.*

The long-lost Helen shows up at the same time as the thief. Both of them have a connection to the inn. Coincidence?

After about twenty minutes, Shannon peered up from the computer screen, rubbing her eyes. "I don't think I'm going to find him in here." She glanced at her watch. "I really need to get back to the shop."

Michael insisted on driving her the short distance down the street to her shop. Once the car was parked, he pushed open his door and strode around to the passenger side, offering Shannon a hand and helping her to the curb. She grabbed the Angel Lewis book Michael had given her with her free hand.

They stood facing each other on the sidewalk outside the store.

He touched the knot on her forehead. "That guy is out there, and now he knows you can identify him."

"I understand." She reached up to ruffle her hair a bit,

trying to cover the bump. "He knows what I look like. It wouldn't take much for him to find out who I am or where I live." Shannon's breath caught in her throat as fear danced across her nerves. "I'll be careful."

"Extra careful." He leaned toward her. "Promise?"

She let out a nervous noise that loosely resembled a laugh. "I promise." After an awkward moment, she turned away and walked toward the shop. She slowed her steps as she reached the door and glanced back over her shoulder. "Michael, thank you for everything you did today."

Color rose up in Michael's cheeks as he waved the compliment away with his hand. "Just looking out for a friend."

"I feel very fortunate to have a friend like you."

"Right back at you." Without another word, he slipped into his car and drove away.

Inside the shop, several customers milled around. Essie emerged from the coffee bar side of the store and greeted Shannon with a warm smile.

"Hey stranger, where have you been all afternoon?"

"It's a long story." Shannon counted half a dozen people in the main part of the store. "How was business after the parade?"

"Steady but not overwhelming." Essie played with the bangles on her wrist.

"Lots of people are probably hitting the craft fair in the park," Shannon said. "I had hoped to get over there myself."

Kristin dusted the counter by the cash register. "My mom came by a while ago. She said it stayed pretty busy over there."

The three women chatted off and on as they worked

through the remainder of the afternoon. When Shannon checked the clock at five thirty, she realized they hadn't had a single customer for over an hour. "I say we close up early."

"Can't argue with you there." Essie perched on a chair stolen from the coffee bar while she flipped through a pattern book. "It's either feast or famine with this festival going on."

"I think that all the festival activities are keeping people away." Shannon moved toward the counter. "Why don't you go have some fun, Kristin? I'll cash out the day's receipts."

Kristin stepped back from the cash register, lifting her chin slightly. Her face turned white as a ghost. "Sure, Mrs. McClain. I'll do that." She pulled off her work apron with the brightly colored Paisley Craft Market logo on it.

If Shannon had been in the business of reading the emotions people were trying to conceal, she would have said that Kristin seemed almost ... afraid. As Kristin exited the shop with a nervous backward glance, the accusations of the cheerleader in the park about missing fundraiser money echoed in Shannon's head.

Essie rose to her feet and stretched. "I could use a long soak in a hot tub."

"That sounds delicious," said Shannon. She pulled the cash from the register and proceeded to count it. "At the parade today, I thought I saw the man who broke into Betty's place. That's what kept me away."

Essie ran a hand through her wild, curly hair. "Did you?"

"Yes, but he got away." Shannon shifted her attention to counting the cash.

"Darn, that's too bad." Essie gathered up her coat and purse from behind the counter.

Shannon placed a ten-dollar bill on top of the pile and glanced up. "How did Kristin do today?"

"She did super." Essie slipped into her animal-print trench coat. "She manned the register for most of the day."

Shannon cringed inwardly. She hated herself for thinking the worst of Kristin, but the other teenager's remarks had made her doubt her own perceptions of people.

Essie stopped at the front door and pounded her forehead with the palm of her hand. "I almost forgot about our special tomorrow." She walked over to the counter where she put down her purse and grabbed a square piece of white board and some markers. While she talked, she proceeded to make a stylish sign advertising that the paint kits were on sale for twenty percent off. Shannon watched with admiration. Only Essie could turn a sales sign into a work of art. In the summer, Essie had made 3-D chalk drawings on the sidewalk to attract customers. Whatever the medium, it seemed Essie was a natural artist.

Essie put the cap on one of the markers. "I know Kristin is only supposed to be temp help, but if you ever need another clerk ... even though she's not particularly craft-oriented, she is good with the customers and so willing to work. Plus, I get the impression she could use really the money."

Shannon managed a slight smile as she put all the checks in a pile and examined the credit card transactions. "I'll keep that in mind."

"You don't think she'd be a good hire?" Essie colored "20% Off" in yellow and orange, adding a flower border at the bottom.

"I hadn't really thought about it." The two women

worked without talking further, the squeaky scratching of the markers on the white board the only sound in the shop.

When Shannon totaled the monies against the cash register, she found everything to be in order. There was no money missing from the register. She could have kick herself for being suspicious. But still, Kristin *had* reacted in a guilty way.

"Everything OK?" Essie sauntered across the shop to position the sign by the paint kits.

Shannon put the money into a bank bag. "Everything's fine, Essie, just fine." She paused. "Sorry, I didn't mean for that to sound so snappy." *The break-in has made me paranoid. Now I'm thinking Helen is connected to it somehow.*

"It's OK." Essie flipped the door sign from "Open" to "Closed." "Oh, I almost forgot to tell you. Your mom called and said she couldn't reach you on your cellphone."

Shannon walked over to where she'd hung her windbreaker. The pocket where she kept her cellphone was empty. "I must've left my phone at home. Did she leave a message?"

"She said she's going to be late getting to your house—something about a chance to sell more food." Essie's clogs pounded on the hardwood floor as she headed across the room to get her purse.

"I suppose she needs to make money when she can."

"Yeah. She probably jumped at a chance to feed people at one of those 'unofficial' concerts in the park tonight put on by a local band," Essie offered.

Shannon checked all the doors to make sure they were locked, and the two women left the shop together. They said their goodbyes, and Essie headed up the street. Shannon could see the town square from the sidewalk, which was still alive with Apple Festival–related activity.

Exhausted, Shannon climbed into Old Blue and drove home. The sky had begun to turn dark blue as she revved up the hill to her home on Larkspur Lane. Her breath caught every time the huge mansion came into view. It still felt like a dream to be living in such a beautiful place.

After parking in the garage, Shannon pushed open the door of her truck and stepped out. Walking around to the other side of the truck, she pushed the button on the garage-door opener on the wall and exited through the side door as the overhead door closed. As she walked toward the front door of the mansion, she glanced at the eastern horizon of the darkening sky where the moon was rising just above a steady, bright point of light that Shannon thought might be the planet Venus. She paused a moment to look up at the twinkling stars that were beginning to appear between the scattered clouds against the midnight-blue expanse and then turned to the west to see the lingering last lights of the setting sun. The prevailing northwest winds were strong and somewhat cold, ruffling her wavy red hair and making her shiver.

She turned around and continued on to the house. She unlocked the front door, and when she was inside the foyer, she walked several steps to set her purse down on the marble table against the wall. When she turned around, the enormous marble statue of a Roman soldier on a black horse rearing up on its legs, its front legs high above a coiled snake, greeted her from its place next to the grand staircase. The nearly two-story-tall statue served as a reminder of her grandmother's eccentric tastes. Though Victoria had remodeled the mansion before her death with Shannon in mind, the older woman certainly had left her mark on the place. Shannon headed toward the kitchen to rustle up some dinner.

On the refrigerator, a magnet held a note from Deborah: *Got invited to do an evening chat on quilting techniques at the inn. Will probably be out late.*

Shannon would have the house all to herself until her mother returned. After the excitement and busyness of the last two days, the solitude was appealing. She warmed up the chicken enchiladas Deborah had left for her and headed to the study.

The study had been her grandmother's favorite place in the house, and it quickly became Shannon's as well. Sometimes the expansiveness of the mansion could be overwhelming. She loved the coziness of the study. The soft, feminine colors and floor-to-ceiling bookshelves welcomed her.

After Shannon finished her dinner, she remembered the Angel Lewis book Michael had given her and ran out to the truck to get it. Back in the study, she nestled into a plush chair and read while the sky turned to pitch black. The book proved to be more interesting than she had anticipated. As a foster-care child, Angel had only lived in Apple Grove for her last two years of high school. She credited her foster parents for encouraging her to pursue her singing dream and said that Apple Grove was the first place she'd been truly happy since being abandoned by her birth mother when she was six.

Shannon looked up from her book to gaze out the window. A sense of uneasiness overtook her when she looked out into the darkness. She was alone in the big house. With the coming of night, it didn't feel so cozy anymore.

It would be easy enough for the dark-haired burglar to find out where she lived. Unable to shake her fear, she jumped to her feet and headed to the foyer. When she peeked outside a front window, she saw no one in the driveway or coming up the road. Her mother wasn't home yet, so she couldn't set the alarm or lock the door and go to bed. Her mother didn't have a key to get in like Deborah did.

Shannon stepped outside and stood on the porch, tuning her ears to the sounds around her. The wind rushed through creaking trees, and masses of dry leaves whirled across the lawn. But nothing out of the ordinary caught her attention.

As a precaution, she went back inside and grabbed a sharp knife from the kitchen before heading upstairs. She checked each of the rooms on the way to her own bedroom.

As she approached the guest bedroom next to hers, a scraping noise reached her ears. She clutched her knife in one hand, and with the other hand, reached around the doorjamb and flipped up the wall light switch. Peering into the room, she realized the sound was coming from outside. She strode to the window, flung it open, and leaned out. Branches of a barren tree brushed against the side of the house in the strong wind.

She'd have to get that thing trimmed. She gazed down at the yard below. No sign of life by the summer house or the lake. The muffled roar of the distant ocean surf was barely audible above the wind.

Shannon quickly checked the other rooms. Relieved to find that she was truly alone in the house, she headed toward her own room to change out of her day clothes. Michael's admonition to be careful was not unfounded. But it had left her spooked. She had the feeling she would be looking over her shoulder until they caught the thief.

Still a little shaken, she brushed her teeth and then prepared to wash her face. Lifting up her hair from her forehead, she could see in the mirror where the dark-haired man had left his mark; she winced as she touched the slightly raised and discolored skin. After she washed her face, she let her hair fall back over the bruise. She changed into her pajamas and headed back downstairs to await her mother's return.

8

"This is way too early for me to be up." Melanie blinked several times and took a sip of her large coffee.

Shannon tied a ribbon around the flowers Melanie had brought from the shop to sell at the booth. "I love early mornings. It's a chance to get things done before the rest of the world wakes up."

Though Melanie could only help for a short while, Shannon planned on staying all day in the Purls' booth. Essie would call Shannon if she were needed at the craft market.

From the booth, Shannon could see the Gourmet on the Go truck across the lawn. She'd awakened to an empty house that morning. Apparently, Beth had left early to get a primo parking spot in the park. Shannon wound the ribbon tightly around the flower stems. Had her mother really come for a visit or was it purely a business decision to attend the festival? Maybe Beth was having financial difficulties and was too embarrassed to say.

"Whoa, you're going to choke the life out of those flowers." Melanie put a hand on Shannon's. She followed the line of Shannon's gaze. "So how is your mom doing these days?"

Shannon placed the flowers into a bucket of water. "Good, as far as I know. I really haven't had much of a chance to visit with her since she's been here."

"You've got time now. We have twenty minutes before the customers start showing up. Go over and talk to her,"

Melanie said. "I can handle the booth if they do come early. Friday is always a slow day anyway."

Shannon tilted her head toward her friend. "Are you sure you don't mind?"

Melanie winked at her. "I mean it. If having cancer has taught me anything, it's that time waits for no one. Seize the moment. When you feel like you should do something, do it."

"You're right. Thanks." Shannon walked across the grass toward the truck. As she approached, a blend of spices, cinnamon, and the saltiness of bacon cooking swirled together and filled the air around her. Shannon peered through the serving window of the truck, but she could only see a small section of her mother's torso.

"Good morning, we won't be serving for about twenty minutes," Beth said without turning. Pots banged together and bacon sizzled.

"Beth, it's me."

"Shannon?" Beth stuck her head through the window and offered Shannon a genuine smile. "Hey, so good to see you! Sorry about running out on you so early this morning. I had a lot to do before the crowds today."

"I understand." Shannon shrugged.

Beth tilted her head, studying Shannon. "How are you doing? Have you had anything to eat yet this morning?"

"A cup of tea. I had to get here early for setup too."

"I saw that. Your booth looks very pretty." Beth leaned further out the window, resting her elbows on the foldout counter. "Why don't you come in, and I'll make you a big breakfast burrito?" Affection emanated from Beth's eyes.

Shannon smiled. "That sounds brilliant."

"Meet me at the back door." Beth disappeared as her footsteps pounded inside the truck.

At the back of the truck, Beth held out a hand to help Shannon up the steps. "You can have the seat of honor." She pointed to a single plastic chair in the corner with a merry laugh.

Shannon sat down in the flimsy chair, which was surprisingly comfortable. She watched her mother break two eggs on the grill.

"You like tomatoes?"

"I like most vegetables," Shannon said.

"You always were a good eater, even when you were a baby."

Shannon watched her mother work with quick efficiency. Beth stood back from the grill for a moment, wiping the sweat from her forehead with the back of her sleeve. She assembled the burrito, placed it on a paper plate with a sliver of orange and parsley garnish, and handed it to her daughter. "Bon appetite."

Beth pulled a large bucket from her wall of supplies, turned it upside down, and used it as a chair.

Shannon savored the first bite—the cheese, veggies, spices, and eggs blended together to create a mouthwatering experience. "This is delicious."

Beth positioned her left elbow on her knee and rested her chin in her hand. "So I heard you witnessed a robbery up at the inn."

"Where did you hear that?"

"Small town—everybody talks, and usually they're talking right in front of the food truck." Beth reached over to a shelf of canned goods and straightened them without rising from her makeshift chair. "A leftover skill from my journalism days is the ability to mentally sort through a bunch of conversations going on at once."

"The rumors are true. I did witness a robbery. Then yesterday, I saw the guy again, so I chased after him." Shannon took another delectable bite of her burrito.

Her mother put her hand over her heart. "Oh Shannon, you could've been hurt—or worse."

Shannon smiled. She liked that her mother expressed so much concern. That would never get old. "The parade occupied the police's attention. I had to do something."

"Did you catch the thief?"

"No, and what's worse is he beaned me on the head with his boot." Shannon lifted a section of thick red hair to reveal the bump.

Beth grimaced. "That looks like it hurt."

"Fortunately, Michael was there to catch me when I fell—literally he caught me—or it could have turned out a lot worse."

Beth raised her eyebrows. "Do you ... like Michael?"

"Well, I ..." Shannon paused. "What makes you ask?"

"The way you say his name." Beth grabbed a paper cup off the counter and took a sip.

"I'm not sure how I feel about him, or how he truly feels about me." Shannon gritted her teeth. "It's complicated." She placed her empty plate on the counter.

Beth played with the strings of her apron. "Men can be hard to understand sometimes—most times."

Shannon laughed in agreement. Beth poured her a glass of orange juice, and they spent a few minutes talking about the twins and the improvements to the craft market and the artists' lofts.

Shannon glanced through the serving window at the street. Three cars pulled up, and several more already filled the parking lot. "Here they come, the consuming masses."

Beth uncrossed her legs and peered through the windows. "I hope they're hungry."

"I'd better get back to our booth." Shannon rose from her chair.

Beth held out her arms and pulled Shannon into a tight hug. "I'm so glad we could spend this time together," she said.

"Me too." Shannon's voice was thick with emotion as she hugged her mother a little tighter.

By the time Shannon got back to the Purls' booth, at least half a dozen patrons were milling around it, admiring the knitted items and other handicrafts.

"Doesn't take long to get swamped," said Melanie as she calculated a purchase for a customer.

"Oh, miss? Does this necklace have matching earrings?" An older woman held up a sterling pendant necklace Shannon had crafted.

"I'm sure we can find something to go with it," Shannon said, stepping toward the jewelry display.

As the day wore on, a steady stream of customers visited the booth, providing no time for Shannon to even sit down for a moment. Melanie left after lunch to return to the flower shop, making Shannon's hope of a break even less likely. As usual, there were more lookers than takers. Many crafters perused festivals to get ideas for their own work rather than to purchase anything. But sales were good enough for Shannon to hope that they'd be able to make a decent donation to cancer research.

By late afternoon, dark clouds filled the sky above the park, threatening rain. Shannon noticed Betty and Helen standing by Joyce's pastry truck; Betty appeared to be introducing Joyce to her sister. After a moment, the two women bid their goodbyes and sauntered toward the Purls' booth.

As they drew near, Shannon noticed Helen deliberately avoiding her gaze. She split off from Betty and wandered over to another booth, while Betty stayed with Shannon.

Shannon rearranged some of the flowers Melanie had brought. "Looks like things are going better for you two."

Betty angled her head slightly to catch a glimpse of Helen two booths away. "Yes, I'm starting to like having my sister back. The workshops are winding down, so I thought we could slip away to at least check out the craft vendors in the park. I hope we can get to some of the other festival activities too." Betty lifted a hand-painted silk scarf from the counter and draped it over her forearm. "I heard you had another close encounter with our burglar yesterday."

Shannon nodded. "Yes, but unfortunately he got away again."

"You know, I *do* think something might be missing from the office. Yesterday, I went into a drawer to get a photo album of the kids to show Helen, and things looked messed up. But I couldn't tell exactly what was missing. I have old photos in the album and some of the kids' things from when they were in school, mostly memorabilia, but there might have been something valuable in there. I just can't remember."

"Hmm ...," said Shannon as she watched Helen converse

with a woman at another booth. "Betty, I have to say something. Please don't take it the wrong way. I think Helen owes you an explanation for where she's been all these years."

Betty's face blanched. "She's hinted at getting into trouble with the law. I don't know exactly what happened. Maybe she'll tell me the details when she feels more comfortable around me."

So Helen had a criminal past, one that might include burglary. Shannon felt torn between wanting to protect her friend from being hurt and wanting to think the best of Helen. *What if I'm wrong in my suspicions?* Betty would feel betrayed. Shannon needed clear evidence that Helen was connected to the robbery—if indeed that was the case.

Shannon offered her friend an encouraging smile. "Yes, these things do take time."

Betty touched Shannon's hand, her eyes filled with warmth. "I knew you'd understand." She picked up the hand-painted silk scarf done in pink and turquoise. "I'd like to buy this for Helen."

Shannon rang up the purchase and watched Betty walk a few booths away to present the scarf to her sister. Helen pressed the scarf to her chest and then took her sister into an awkward hug.

There's something odd about Helen's demeanor ....

A teenage boy picked up a knitted hat and glove set and pulled Shannon from her thoughts when he asked, "I want to buy something for my girlfriend. Do you think this would be nice but not too over the top?"

Shannon stayed busy the rest of the day as the wind blew and the sky grew darker. Several of her regular local customers stopped by to say hello. The constant line at Gourmet on the Go indicated that her mother probably wouldn't have a free moment all day.

"You look like you're starving to death, kiddo." Joyce stood in front of her, holding a paper plate topped with a pink-and-green frosted cupcake. The pink frosting was almost as intense as Joyce's trademark fuchsia lipstick.

"Joyce, I'm going to weigh three hundred pounds before this is all over."

"You're a skinny-minny. You could use some meat on your bones, so eat up." Joyce placed one hand on her ample hip, which caused the metal bracelets she wore to jangle.

"Yes, boss lady." Shannon picked up the cupcake, her mouth watering. She took a single bite just as lightning flashed and thunder crackled in the sky.

Joyce tilted her head up, her expression growing grim. "Maybe we'll only get a light sprinkling."

"If we're lucky." Shannon retrieved plastic bags from her truck and placed them over the hand-painted scarves and knitted items that weren't under the canopy of the booth. A few drops landed on her arms as she worked. Without warning, the sprinkles turned into a deluge, like a bucket being emptied from the sky.

People raced to their cars and toward the shelter of the downtown shops using purses and hands as makeshift umbrellas.

Booth owners frantically tried to cover their merchandise. Shannon grabbed one of the plastic tubs they'd brought the inventory in. "This stuff won't survive this much water."

Joyce slipped behind the counter. "I can help you. The

Sprinkles truck is waterproof. It will only take my employees a second to pack up the pastries on display."

The crowds thinned as other booth owners scrambled to save their handicrafts from the downpour. Shannon and Joyce moved at a fast pace to pack up as much as they could. Despite the speed at which they worked and how soaked they were, Shannon laughed.

Joyce laughed too, wiping the rain from her forehead. "This is crazy."

"Here, let me help you with that." Matthew, the part-time loft renter and full-time welder, appeared at their side and reached out for one of the plastic tubs. "You want this taken to your truck cab, right?"

"Yes, thank you. What about your own stuff?" Shannon gathered up the knitted crafts first, clutching them close to her chest as she raced to the plastic tub.

"My sculptures were made to be put in gardens," Matthew said. "They'll be fine."

Within five minutes, the cab of Shannon's truck was packed up. "The booth should be OK. It's pretty weatherproof." She said goodbye to Matthew and Joyce. "Thanks for all your help."

As Shannon turned the key in the ignition, Betty ran up to the side of Old Blue, her hair soaked and stringy from the downpour, her expression frantic.

Shannon opened her door. "What's wrong?"

Betty wiped the moisture off her forehead. "Have you seen Helen? I can't find her anywhere."

"No." Wind gusted around Shannon. "Did you all walk or drive here?"

Betty crossed her arms over her chest. "We drove."

"Maybe she ran back to the inn when she saw the storm moving in."

"I suppose." Betty glanced around at the few people still darting for shelter or dealing with flimsy booths blowing across the park. "It seems strange that she didn't try to find me."

"I bet she's back at the inn, safe and warm," Shannon assured Betty, even as her own suspicions rose to the surface. Something had not been right about Helen from the moment of her arrival, and now she had vanished. Again.

"You're probably right. I'd better get back to the inn and check." The worry lines in Betty's forehead remained. She turned and trotted back toward her car.

Before Shannon could shut her door, she heard someone call her name.

She stuck her head out of the truck once more and saw Beth jogging across the grass, waving her hand. While she was still some distance away, she shouted, "This is some crazy storm!"

"I know!" Shannon shouted back.

"You heading home now?"

"Yes."

Beth shaded her eyes from the rain though her clothes were already soaked. "I'll meet you back at the house."

"See you there." Shannon drove with the rain pelting her hood and the wipers doing their best to slap the windshield clear. She looked forward to building a fire and sipping cocoa with her mother.

She only hoped Betty would have the same kind of cozy afternoon with her sister.

— 9 —

"She's not here." Stress permeated Betty's voice across the telephone line.

Holding the phone to her ear, Shannon pivoted slightly and glanced at Deborah and Beth seated by the fire, eating scones and sipping cocoa. "Oh dear," Shannon said. "Where could she have gone? She doesn't have a car."

"Tom said I should give her a few more hours. She might be waiting out the rain." Betty sucked in an audible breath. "But I'm worried. I have this terrible feeling something's not right."

"You don't get any answer when you try her cellphone?"

Deborah and Beth must have picked up on Shannon's worried tone. They both rose from their chairs near the fireplace and hovered a few feet away from her.

"I didn't even know she *owned* a cellphone." Betty sounded as though she was going to cry. "She certainly never offered to give me the number."

Shannon recalled the cellphone conversation she'd overheard when Helen had hid in the trees some distance from the inn, obviously not wanting to be overheard. Maybe Helen finally decided that getting reacquainted with her baby sister had "all been too much" and had left town. *But how?* "Did Helen ever mention a husband or children?"

"She said her husband was dead, and that she has one daughter who lives in England."

To whom had Helen been talking on the phone that day? Again, Shannon thought of the thief and the coincidence of both of them showing up on the same day. "Maybe she told you something that will give us a clue. Think about all of your conversations. You said she mentioned something about being in trouble with the law."

"She told me she got in trouble for writing bad checks." Betty's voice trembled. "I figured she would tell me more once she felt comfortable. I thought we'd have more time."

"Did she say anything that seemed out of character or … odd?"

Betty's words came slowly as though she were mulling over everything Helen had said or done. "No … no." A heavy pause settled between them. "Wait. One thing she did seemed weird to me."

"What's that?"

"She wanted to help quite a bit with the work we did running the inn. I really appreciated that. She arrived at this busy time, and she jumped in and dealt with guests. She was really helpful, but when I suggested that the best way she could help would be to teach a quilting class … she got irritated."

Shannon bit her lower lip. Why would the simple request anger Helen? The strange reaction only reinforced Shannon's suspicions about the woman. It *was* a little weird that a master quilter wouldn't want to teach a class, but it wasn't really information that would help them find Helen. Poor Betty sounded so distressed. They had to do something. Outside, the rain sprinkled rather than poured. No lightning flashed across the darkening sky. "Betty, here's what we're going to do. I'm going to try and reach as many of the Purls as I can. We'll all meet at the park and see if we can retrace Helen's steps."

"Oh thank you, Shannon. I don't mean to push the panic button. I'm sure there's a reasonable explanation for wherever she is." Betty sounded like she was trying to convince herself more than anything. "Do you think we should call Chief Grayson?"

"His hands will be tied as to what he can do—a person's not really considered 'missing' if they've only been gone a few hours. It would be a good idea to let him know, but let's search first."

Shannon didn't need to press to know that they were both thinking the same thing. The most reasonable explanation was that Helen had left town.

Within half an hour Shannon, Beth, Joyce, and Betty all gathered in the park. Each held an umbrella as a smattering of rain continued to fall. The park, once alive with colorful booths and excited crowds, looked like something out of an apocalyptic movie under the early evening sky. The booths that vendors hadn't had time to take down now drooped from the weight of the rain, and torn canvas booth covers flapped in the wind.

The women stood in a tight circle, each trying to remember when they had last seen Helen.

"Was she wearing a brown dress and a hat?" Joyce turned from side to side, taking in the whole park which was illuminated by the lampposts scattered throughout. "'Cause I saw a woman wearing that running toward those trees earlier." She pointed with her flashlight to the dark grove of gnarled apple trees on the park's periphery.

Betty shook her head. "No, her dress was blue. We bought it today. We went shopping together."

"You know, I do remember seeing a woman in a blue dress walking toward the edge of the park, toward the old apple orchard," Beth said. "I think it was right before the rain got so intense and people started to pack up. I don't remember seeing a woman in a brown dress, though. That must have been when I started to pack up."

"Maybe she ran into the orchard to get out of the rain and lost her way. I don't know what's on the other side of those trees. Let's spread out and see what we can find. The trail leads this way," Shannon said, clicking on her flashlight.

Betty followed behind Shannon while Joyce and Beth veered off the trail.

The trees grew thicker and the path more wild, creating a dark covering overhead. "Where does this trail lead?" Shannon asked Betty.

Because they possessed only one flashlight between them, Betty pressed close to Shannon's shoulder. "I don't know. I've never gone walking through here. It looks like the closer we get to the woods and away from the apple trees, there's not really a trail to follow."

As the trees became more dense and tangled, Shannon tried to pick a path through the brush that a person would most likely walk.

Shouts sounded from somewhere in the woods.

"That sounds like Joyce," Betty said, gripping Shannon's arm.

Joyce repeated something over and over. Gradually, it became clear what she was saying. "We found something!"

"Over here!" shouted Shannon.

Branches creaked and cracked as Joyce and Beth pushed through the forest.

Joyce emerged first, holding a lump in her hand. "Does this look familiar?"

Shannon shone a light on a gossamer cloth, now soaked with rain.

Betty gasped. "That's the silk scarf I bought for Helen today."

"We found it hanging on a branch," Beth said.

"She draped it around her neck after I gave it to her." Betty lifted the soggy scarf from Joyce's hand. "It could have fallen off if she ran in here to get out of the rain earlier."

"Why in the world would she run into the trees during a storm with lightning?" Shannon asked, shaking her head. "At least we know she came this way. Take me back to where you found the scarf, Joyce."

As she followed behind Joyce and Beth, Shannon noticed several broken branches, damage that could have been done by the storm … or by someone in a hurry to get through the trees. *What was Helen doing out here?* The flashlight beam made the rain on the leaves glisten as Shannon searched around. Her gaze landed on something shiny in the underbrush, and she kneeled to pick it up.

"What is it?" Beth appeared beside her as she rose to her feet.

Shannon shone the flashlight on the tiny metal object. "A teddy bear. It looks like a charm from a bracelet."

Joyce turned around to face the others. "That could've been dropped at any time."

"True," said Shannon. All the same, she put the charm in her jacket pocket and zipped it shut. "Let's see if we can figure out which way Helen went."

The beam from the flashlight bobbed as they pushed through the trees and stepped out onto a dirt road.

Across the road stood a line of small, older homes. Located outside the city limits, the homes were known to be less-expensive rentals.

"If she did take this path, what happened to her?" Betty's voice held a haunted tone.

A porch light came on across the street. The door opened and a small dog darted out, followed by a woman. Shannon thought the woman looked familiar. *Kristin's mom.*

"I know that lady. I'll ask her if she's seen anyone around here today fitting Helen's description." Shannon jogged across the road. She waved and shouted, "Sissy!"

Sissy approached the fence. Recognition spread across her face as Shannon drew closer.

"Mrs. McClain, what on earth brings you out on a night like this?"

Shannon stood for a moment, trying to catch her breath. "A friend of mine." She turned back toward where the other three women huddled under umbrellas. "Her sister is visiting, and she didn't come home after the storm. We're a little concerned. We think she walked through the trees out to this road."

Sissy put her hands on her hips. "What did she look like?"

"Older woman, mid- to late sixties, tall. She was wearing a blue dress."

The little dog bounded across the lawn and sat at Sissy's feet. "Does she have health problems?"

That was something Shannon hadn't considered. "Not as far as I know. We last saw her in the park. I don't suppose you noticed anyone walking on this road today? Or maybe a strange car? It would have been right around the time the storm hit."

Sissy chewed her lower lip as she considered the question. "I stayed in town for hours, enjoying the festivities. Kristin, as you know, was at your shop most of the day." Sissy turned toward the row of houses that lined the road. "Maybe somebody else noticed something."

"I don't want to bother them this late at night. Thank you." She turned to go, but then turned back. "Where is Kristin?"

Sissy placed her hands on her hips. "That kid doesn't like to spend much time at home. She's at a friend's house."

Shannon thanked Sissy again and headed back across the road where the other women waited. "She doesn't know anything that can help us."

"This road doesn't look very busy. Someone probably would have noticed if a strange car had come by here," Beth commented.

"Most everyone hung out in town today, though." Shannon said.

"We can't do any more tonight." Betty's voice dropped almost to a whisper as she bent her head.

"We can call Grayson and tell him what we found," Joyce offered. "He can question the people in those houses if she doesn't show up or call soon."

Betty nodded. "OK. At least that's something."

Joyce wrapped an arm around Betty. "Shannon, why don't you and Beth go home? Betty and I will deal with talking to the police. It's been a long day already."

"Are you sure?" Shannon was bone tired, but worried about Betty as well.

"We'll be fine." Joyce sounded robust and rested as ever.

Shannon appreciated how the Purls found ways to carry each other's emotional burdens.

The women trudged back through the trees, pushing branches aside and stepping over underbrush. Once they were in the park, Shannon and Beth returned to her truck. Shannon slipped in behind the wheel and shoved the key into the ignition.

Beth rested her head against the back of the cab. "What a night, huh?"

"I'll say." A thousand thoughts tumbled through Shannon's head. What happened to Helen? She'd seemed happy enough at the park—from afar at least. According to Betty it sounded as if they were working through issues. Shannon sighed. "I really need to clear my head. I find a drive up the coast always helps. Do you mind? I could drop you off at the house if you don't want to go."

"No, that sounds like a great idea," Beth said. "It looks like the rain is going to let up."

Within minutes, the old blue Ford sped up the coast. The rain had dwindled to a sprinkle, and Shannon opened her window to let in the cleansing scent of the salt air.

"I miss this part of the world sometimes. Portland can get so busy and stuffy." Beth turned her head and gazed out her window.

A comfortable silence fell between them. Shannon turned the wheel into a curve as the headlights ate up the yellow line on the highway. An SUV loomed behind them. They entered a curvy part of the two-lane highway, and the driver of the SUV stayed so close that all Shannon could see in her rearview mirror were headlights.

"Do you think Helen left town?" Shannon asked.

Her mother thought about it for a moment. "I never met Helen, and I don't know Betty that well. Forty-five years is a long time. People can change a lot in—"

A sudden tap to the bumper of the truck made it lurch. Shannon let out a cry and gripped the steering wheel tighter.

"What on earth?" Beth craned her neck to look through the back glass. "That SUV is right on top of us. Do you think he's drunk?"

The engine of the SUV roared behind them, and it collided with the back bumper again, this time more forcefully. The truck swerved slightly, and Shannon fought to gain control of the wheel.

The first tap might have been written off as a fluke of inattentive driving, but the second collision indicated the driver's ill intent.

Beth braced her hand against the metal dashboard. "He's trying to run us off the road!"

Shannon pressed the accelerator to the floor. The truck topped out at sixty-five.

The SUV, a newer model, zoomed up beside them and slammed hard against the side of the truck. Old Blue careened toward the edge of the road, coming close to a cluster of evergreens.

Her heart pounding, Shannon gripped the wheel. "I can't outrun him!"

The driver hit them again. Two times. Three times. The front end of the truck wobbled as the back end swung out from behind. Cascading images of rocks and road passed in front of Shannon as the dark metal of the vehicle aimed to ram them again.

— 10 —

The final collision caused Old Blue to veer toward the trees. Shannon overcorrected the steering wheel. The truck swerved across the road, bumped over a stretch of rocks, and skidded to stop on the sand by the ocean. The engine sputtered and then died altogether.

With her heart racing, Shannon cranked the key. "It won't start."

Beth grabbed her daughter's forearm. "I think we have bigger problems than that."

Shannon jerked her head toward the road where the dark SUV had stopped. Fear tainted Shannon's words. "Is he coming down here to finish us off?"

"I wouldn't take any bets on that," Beth said. "Let's get out of here!"

Shannon pushed the lever to open her door, but it wouldn't budge. "My door is smashed in! I can't open it."

Beth opened her door and tugged on Shannon's sleeve. "This way. We'll have to run up the beach."

Beth climbed out and crouched by the truck. Shannon followed. Staying low to the ground, they hurried around the back end of truck. With the truck positioned between them and the SUV on the road, Shannon dared to lift her head above the truck bed to see if the driver had gotten out.

The SUV's door opened. In the dim light, she could

discern only the vague silhouette of the driver. She couldn't say for sure if the figure was male or female.

"We'll have a pretty good head start on him," Beth said.

Unless he has a gun.

A second car heading toward Apple Grove drove by. The car slowed and then stopped all together. The driver's door opened, and a man stepped out, his yellow shirt visible in the evening light. He waved his arms at them and shouted, but the tide and wind drowned out his words. The man stalked toward them on the beach and shouted again.

The driver of the SUV slipped back into his vehicle and sped away.

As the man drew closer, his bright, friendly face eased Shannon's fear. The women ran out to meet him on the rocky shore. The yellow shirt the man wore offset his blond, curly hair and deep tan. He looked vaguely familiar, though Shannon couldn't quite place him.

"Looks like you folks had an accident." He stared up the highway where darkness swallowed the black SUV. "Why didn't that other guy stop to help? Or is he the reason for your accident?"

Shannon didn't want to explain the traumatic last few minutes of her life to a stranger. "It's a long story."

The man pointed toward Old Blue. "Is your truck in any condition to drive?"

Shannon and Beth shook their heads in unison.

"It won't start," Shannon said.

"Where are you headed?"

"Apple Grove."

The man turned back toward the road. "I'm headed that

way myself. I can give you a ride into town."

Shannon's hands still shook from her near-death experience, and she wasn't sure her heart would ever slow down to normal. The man's offer of help, though, filled her with gratitude and calmed her frayed nerves. "Thank you."

He leaned a little closer to Shannon. "Now I know where I've seen you. You own that craft shop downtown. I'm Hunter Banks. You gave me directions to the house rental agency the other day. I'm moving to Apple Grove to do ocean research."

"Oh, yeah." She had only a foggy memory of him, but didn't want to hurt his feelings. He was being so nice.

Beth stepped in. "We're so thankful you stopped."

"Come on back to the car. Let's get you ladies home, safe and sound. We'll get that truck taken care of too—you can look up the number for a towing company on my phone."

Shannon slipped into the backseat, and to her surprise Beth climbed in beside her, wrapping her arms around her daughter.

Hunter settled in behind the steering wheel. "Now you're going to make me feel like a chauffeur."

"Forgive us," said Beth. "I think the accident frightened both of us silly." She pulled Shannon a little closer.

Hunter nodded in understanding. "Maybe I should take you two to the hospital?"

"I think we'd just like to go home," said Shannon. "We'll be all right."

Beth carried on a conversation with Hunter as the horror of what they'd experienced replayed in Shannon's mind.

Before Hunter pulled away from the shoulder, he checked his phone for the number of a local towing service.

He repeated the phone number to Shannon who made the call. After she clicked off her phone, she stared out the window while Hunter did most of the talking.

His work as a marine biologist had brought him to Apple Grove to study rockfish diets. He enjoyed the festival, and Apple Grove seemed like a nice place to live.

As he drove, Hunter talked and Beth offered one-word responses, but images of the assault from the SUV continued to bombard Shannon. She closed her eyes. They were safe now. She had to let it go.

She looked down at the phone she still gripped in her hand. The thought came into her head that she wanted to talk to Michael, to tell him what had happened. She suspected that the SUV driver and the burglar were one and the same. Now that he knew she could identify him, he wanted her gone. *But why? Betty wasn't even sure what had been taken from her office. What does she have at the inn worth killing for?*

Shannon returned to her presumption that Helen and the thief were connected. What if Helen wanted out of whatever scheme they planned to carry out? Maybe she possessed a little bit of a conscience, and she didn't want to hurt her sister again. Shannon rubbed her tired eyes. All she could do was speculate. She didn't know anything for sure—she had no proof.

"... I owe a debt to the National Science Foundation for sponsoring this study."

While Shannon was lost in her thoughts, Hunter chattered on without Shannon really comprehending what he was talking about.

"Yes, that's a good thing ..." Shannon replied absently,

hoping that it was. Her voice trailed off as she gazed at the passing landscape. The ocean below was shrouded in darkness, its waves crashing against the shore. Again the feelings returned of being tossed and banged around in the truck, of being helpless to stop it, and she shuddered.

As though she'd read Shannon's mind, Beth put a warm hand on her daughter's shoulder. Shannon patted Beth's hand, thankful that she didn't have to go through the ordeal alone.

*　　*　　*

The next morning, Saturday, Shannon borrowed Deborah's car to drive to work at the craft market. When she called the auto shop mechanic, he told her it would only take an afternoon to get Old Blue running. If she wasn't too picky about appearances, he could pound out the dent that made the driver's-side door stick. Shannon laughed at the remark in spite of herself. Old Blue displayed such an abundance of dents, peeling paint, and rust that one more bit of damage would only add to the truck's character.

Once the flurry of customers died down, Shannon slipped out of her apron and informed Kristin and Essie that she needed to go to the police station.

Her meeting with Grayson proved frustrating. As she talked to the chief, she realized she had very little to offer in terms of catching the person who had run them off the road. She couldn't say for sure why it had happened. She couldn't identify the perpetrator as either a man or woman, and the SUV was a very generic model.

Grayson listened without interrupting, but then said, "This might be a random incident by some fruitcake on the highway. I can check and see if anyone else reported a similar incident."

Shannon shifted in the chair opposite him, growing more upset. "My instinct tells me that the same person who robbed the inn tried to run me off the road."

Grayson rested his elbows on the desk and leaned toward her. "What makes you think the two incidents are connected?"

"That guy knows I can identify him." She lifted her chin and sat up a little straighter. She knew Grayson dealt in material evidence, but there was something to be said for deductive reasoning and gut feelings.

Grayson leaned back in his chair, making it creak. "We don't even have a clear idea what he took from the inn ... if anything. And now you want me to believe the guy is willing to kill for it?"

"Betty said the drawers where she kept photo albums and personal things looked like they'd been disturbed," Shannon said.

"So you think this thief took a million-dollar photograph that Betty didn't even know she owned."

As Shannon ignored Grayson's sarcasm, a realization dawned. "No, he must not have gotten what he wanted. Otherwise he would have left town after the office burglary. He stayed in town for a reason."

Grayson leaned back in his chair and placed his feet on his desk, crossing them at the ankle. "And that reason is?"

Shannon jumped to her feet. She was getting nowhere with Grayson. "I can't prove it yet, but I think the burglary and my being run off the road are connected ... and I wonder if Helen's mysterious arrival isn't somehow tied into all of it."

Grayson drew his eyebrows together and crossed his arms over his chest. Clearly, he did not think much of her theory. "And what about Helen's disappearance?"

"I don't know yet, but I'll figure it out." She turned and walked toward the door.

Grayson's words pelted her back like a spray of bullets. "Now hold on just a minute. *You'll* figure it out? Don't you mean the *police* will figure it out?"

Shannon didn't answer—she simply glanced back and smiled.

As she strolled back to the craft market, the cool fall morning lifted her spirits. The sky was clear blue with no dark clouds in sight. The downtown bustled with people crowding in and out of the shops.

She walked past Michael's office, half expecting and half hoping to see him through the window. There were no lights on inside, but she could make out a man standing behind Michael's computer where the glow of the screen lit up the figure with his head bent low. Shannon tapped on the glass. The man raised his head.

Dylan.

Though he acknowledged her with a nod, something about his expression carried guilt, at least in Shannon's estimation. He backed away from the window into the dark interior of the office. Such a strange response fed her mistrust of him. She recalled his bizarre explanation for lurking upstairs at the inn—that he was looking at some part of the security system in the supply closet.

Certainly, Michael of all people must do a detailed background check on everyone he hires. Her hand wrapped around the knob of the office door as she tried to turn it, but it was locked. Was Dylan even supposed to be in Michael's office?

Her curiosity piqued, Shannon moved on down the street toward the Paisley Craft Market.

Essie opened the door for her. She wore her usual flowing skirt and billowing lacey blouse. "Beth called."

Beth had left the mansion early in her food truck to catch the breakfast crowd at the park. Shannon hadn't had a chance to talk to her since their wild ride the previous night.

No doubt her mother had probably recovered from the incident fine. Beth demonstrated a kind of steel spine in the face of danger, a personality trait which had made her such a great investigative journalist. "What did she say?"

"She told me about what happened last night. She suggested if it was at all possible, I should get you to take the day off."

"But don't you need my help?" Shannon asked, turning a half-circle.

Essie tilted her head and crossed her arms over her chest. "How much of this festival have you actually gotten to enjoy?"

"Well, I—"

"Exactly. If you're not chasing down thieves, you're running workshops or manning the booth. Today is the best and last full day of the festival. They've got all kinds of stuff going on in the town square, and there's the concert tonight." Essie placed her hands on Shannon's shoulders and twirled her around. "Go. Enjoy yourself. This is your first Apple Festival, and you've spent all your time working."

"What if the shop gets busy? When is Kristin scheduled to be on shift?"

"She'll get here soon enough." Essie waved the concern away with her hand. "I'll grab one of the artists from upstairs to give me a hand and pay them out of petty cash if we get swamped."

Reluctantly, Shannon stepped back out into the sunshine just as Kate was parking her car with the Ultimutt Grooming sign on it. Betty sat in the passenger seat. She turned toward Shannon, her face drawn with despair.

Kate slipped out of the car. "We're just swinging by to get coffee at Espresso Yourself and to say hi before heading to the park to take over the booth."

"Essie will be glad to make you whatever you want," Shannon said. "I've been instructed to go and 'enjoy' the best day of the festival."

Betty opened the car door and stepped out onto the sidewalk. Dull eyes stared back at Shannon. Betty looked like she hadn't slept in a week. Shannon didn't need to ask if Helen had returned. Betty's demeanor told her everything she needed to know.

"Looks like it's going to be a sunny day," Kate said, stepping around the front of the car to stand on the sidewalk with her friends. Her cheerfulness seemed a little forced, as though she were trying to use positive small talk to keep Betty from falling apart. "We should have some good sales at the booth. All those people who have been looking for three days will finally decide to buy something."

Shannon's heart flooded with compassion as she patted Betty's arm. "How are you holding up?"

"I'm a little numb." Betty stared at the sidewalk. "I think it's pretty clear she's left town without even saying goodbye."

"Are you sure you feel up to sitting in the booth all day?"

"It'll get my mind off of things. Most of the guests from the workshops are staying on through the end of the festival, so we don't have any new check-ins. Tom said he could handle it."

"I would be glad to step in if you change your mind," Shannon said. "Essie is insisting I take the day off from the shop to enjoy the apple festivities."

"Essie is right," Kate said. "You need a break, and the festival is a lot of fun."

"I suppose."

Kate turned toward Betty. "How about I go inside and get our coffees?"

Shannon took advantage of their moment alone to talk with Betty. "I know this is hard for you."

"I feel so guilty for being angry with her over not finding me sooner. Maybe she picked up on that." Betty's voice faltered. "Maybe I drove her away."

"Don't do this to yourself. Those feelings were normal, given the circumstance. You're a kind and loving person. I know this is a hard thing to deal with, but maybe Helen left because she needed to sort through all her feelings."

And maybe she got cold feet over whatever she had cooked up with the thief.

Betty pressed Shannon's upper arm. "But what if she never calls or comes back?"

"She will. Her emotions are probably so mixed up right now. She'll be in touch," Shannon assured.

"She took off so quickly, like she did it on impulse. She only had one small suitcase, and she left that behind."

Shannon frowned. "That does seem odd. Maybe we should open her suitcase to see if we can find some clue about how to get in touch with her."

Betty shook her head. "I couldn't go through her private things. And besides, I think doing that might upset her more if I do find her or she returns on her own. She obviously left because being with me was too painful."

"You don't know that for sure," Shannon said.

Kate came out of the store holding two cups. "I got yours with a shot of vanilla like you like, Betty."

Shannon said goodbye to the women and headed up the sidewalk. Still puzzling over Helen's strange disappearance, Shannon crossed the street to the town square. The boom of the high school band grew louder. The town square featured a series of booths and a small stage. As she arrived, a group of children ran past her holding balloons advertising various local businesses. The layout featured an area for apple bobbing and a long table set up for cooks to bring apple pies and preserves to be judged in a contest.

As she took in the bright colors and the sense of fun, she couldn't help but wish one of the Purls or Beth could join her to enjoy the festivities.

"Looks like a blast, doesn't it?"

Michael slipped beside Shannon. The navy button-down shirt he wore brought out the blue of his eyes.

"Oh, Michael. I was just thinking about you a little bit ago."

He regarded her, showing keen interest. "Really?"

"Yes, I walked by your office this morning and saw Dylan standing by your desk in the dark. It struck me as odd."

Michael's expression hardened. "Nothing odd about it. He does work for me."

Something in Michael's guarded response warned her she shouldn't pry anymore. She heeded the warning—it was too beautiful a day to be getting into disagreements with him. "What do you have on your schedule for the morning?" she asked.

He looked at his watch. "Not much, believe it or not. Angel Lewis had to make an appearance on a Portland television show. My contract with her only covers the time she's in Apple Grove. She'll be back later for the book signing and, of course, the concert tonight."

Shannon nodded. "Yes, the book. I started reading it. Angel's had a harder life than I realized. Her mother abandoned her at a young age."

"It's surprising what you learn about people sometimes." Michael looked at her intently. "So this is your first Apple Festival?"

"It is."

"Why don't I show you the ropes?" He had a sort of twinkle in his gaze that made her legs wobbly.

"OK, lead the way."

Shannon thought it would be nice to see a more relaxed and lighthearted side of Michael for a change, a side she hadn't seen in what seemed like ages. She decided against telling him about being run off the road. No doubt that would cause him to swing back into his overprotective, tense mode.

As they walked, he wrapped his arm through hers as

though it were the most natural thing in the world. "The first thing we should try is an applesauce Popsicle."

She chuckled. "A *what*?"

"Just wait—you're going to love it."

He led her to a tent with chairs and tables set up. Behind a counter, several women dressed in colorful aprons waited to serve them. The menu board featured predictable dishes like apple cake, pie, and cobbler, but it also included more surprising fare like apple garlic chicken and apple smoothies.

Michael bought them each an applesauce Popsicle. Shannon took a bite, not sure what to expect. A cool explosion of cinnamon and sweet apple filled her mouth.

"Mmmm. This is heavenly."

He grinned. "Told you."

They strolled around the festival grounds. At one booth, kids played apple-themed games; at another, a man demonstrated carving apple tree wood. At the gazebo, the mayor introduced the apple queen, and she sang a number to the band's accompaniment. As Shannon listened to the young woman sing, she could feel someone, somewhere, staring at her. Nervously, she glanced around.

Michael leaned toward her. "Something wrong?"

"I ..." She shook her head. Last night had spooked her. She needed to let it go. "It's nothing. Probably my imagination working overtime." She laced her arm through Michael's. "Let's go see what kind of trouble we can get ourselves into."

As they wandered around, Shannon felt the tension drain from her muscles. They stopped to watch the mayor and his staff plant an apple tree in the town square. The mayor jumped on the shovel with both feet in an effort to break up the earth. Finally, he gave up, handing the shovel over to the brawny man standing next to him.

Michael leaned close to Shannon and whispered in her ear, "This happens every year."

Shannon suppressed a laugh. She counted ten apple trees surrounding the town square. "If they do this every year, there should be an orchard here by now."

"Most of the trees die. No one knows why other than rotten luck. It's really just a ceremonial part of the festival's tradition."

"Ah," Shannon said. "Traditions are good."

"I agree; that's why I think we should try our hand, or should I say, our heads at bobbing for apples." Michael pointed to an area set off with ribbon featuring metal tubs of water and baskets filled with red and green apples.

Shannon held up her hand in protest and shook her head. "Oh no, you're not getting me to do that."

"Come on. It's *tradition*." Michael grinned and grabbed her by the hand. He directed her toward the metal washtubs filled with water and apples. The sign advertised that it cost a dollar to bob for three apples, and that all proceeds were to go to the local elementary school.

A little girl of about seven strutted over to them. "What kind of apple would you like to bob for? We have Granny Smith, Red Delicious and ..." The little girl wrinkled her forehead and looked at the sky. "And um ..." She turned toward a woman who was helping another child fill a tub with apples. "What's the third kind of apples we have?"

"Pink Lady," said the woman, who was probably a grade school teacher or a mom.

The little girl planted her feet and gazed up at them. "Pink Lady."

"Pink Lady sounds wonderful." Michael opened his wallet and pulled out a twenty.

The little girl's eyes grew wide. "Wow, thanks!" She turned toward Shannon. "You might want to tie back your hair. We have ribbons on the table for you to use if you want."

Shannon picked up a green ribbon. She gathered her thick hair into her fingers but dropped the ribbon when she attempted to tie it back.

Michael stepped toward her, kneeling to pick up the ribbon. "Here, let me help you with that."

She felt a tug as he drew the ribbon underneath her hair and tied it up. His fingers grazed her neck.

"How's that?" His voice held that soft smolder again.

Shannon's heartbeat quickened. She touched the back of her head where she felt a neat bow. "It'll do."

Despite her wet face, Shannon found herself laughing as she dunked under water to chase a Pink Lady. She came up with the apple in her teeth.

Michael took it out of her mouth and tossed it in the bucket with the other used apples. He offered her a towel to dry her face and gave her an endearing smile. "I'd say you're a pro."

"What's going to happen to all those apples with bite marks in them?"

"We donate them to a local pig farmer," the teacher who was supervising explained.

Shannon said, "I'm glad they don't go to waste." Just then, her phone buzzed, and she took it out of her purse. It was a text from Essie.

Don't stop having fun. I need to know what you did with the shipment of scrapbooking materials.

Michael leaned toward her. "Something important?"

Shannon stared at her phone screen. It would be easier to go get the supplies for Essie than try to describe via text where they were. "I think I'd better return to the shop."

"I understand. Real life calls. I've got a few things I should probably check up on at the office."

She turned to face Michael and smiled broadly. "I had a lovely time this morning. Thanks for making my first Apple Festival memorable."

"Thank *you* for teaching me a thing or two about how to bob for apples." Michael grinned. "I'll walk with you as far as my office."

As they wove through the clusters of people, Shannon once again had the feeling of being watched. She studied the faces in the crowd as she pushed through, her heart rate kicking into high gear. But no one stood out as suspicious.

Shannon and Michael stepped onto a side street, and the noise of the festivities in the town square diminished. They walked along the road in silence, until they passed a large warehouse —where a woman's terrified scream cut through the air.

— 11 —

Melanie emerged from the warehouse, eyes flashing crazily from side to side. Fear colored her features.

Shannon and Michael intercepted her. "Melanie! What on earth …"

Melanie opened her mouth to speak, but no words came out. Her eyes were wide with terror.

Shannon grabbed Melanie's trembling hands. "Take a deep breath."

Melanie gulped in air. "I was in the warehouse. It's where we parked the float after the parade. I wanted to take some photos 'cause the ones from the parade didn't come out very good, and …" Her breath hitched, and she closed her eyes.

Several people on the outskirts of the festival who'd heard the scream hurried over to them.

Not wanting Melanie to get more agitated, Shannon said in a gentle voice, "It's OK. Tell me what happened."

"There's a … I saw a …" Melanie shuddered.

"Melanie, whatever happened, it's all right," Michael said, growing visibly more impatient and concerned. "You can tell us."

"The skirt on the float was torn. I bent down and lifted it to fix it. Oh heavens to Betsy, there's a dead woman beneath the float!" She spat her words out in rapid-fire fashion. "I couldn't see her face, but I saw enough of the woman to know she's dead."

Within minutes, the mayor and Chief Grayson had arrived on the scene. Shannon told them what Melanie had said, and Grayson and the mayor raced into the warehouse.

One of the officers took up a post in front of the door after Grayson entered. The deputy spoke to the gathering crowd: "You folks need to move along. The police have this matter well in hand."

Shannon remained on the sidewalk, close to Melanie. A young girl brought her a cup of water.

"Has the float been in there since the parade ended?" Michael asked.

"Yes. The place is unlocked. Anybody could have gone inside." Melanie's voice wavered.

Shannon furled her forehead at Michael, hoping to communicate that he should quit his line of questioning. Talking about what she'd seen wouldn't calm Melanie down. Understanding her signal, Michael stepped back.

Melanie took a sip of water, closed her eyes, and then said something under her breath Shannon couldn't quite understand.

Shannon leaned a little closer. "Melanie, did you say something?"

The words came out in a harsh whisper. "It was such a horrible sight. Her blue dress was torn."

Blue dress. Shannon felt as if the blood in her veins had turned to ice. *Helen.*

Grayson emerged from the warehouse, looking pale. Shannon ran over to meet him.

"Is it an older woman in a blue dress?"

Grayson nodded.

Even as she spoke, Shannon could feel herself going numb. "Based on what Melanie told me, I think it might be Betty's missing sister, Helen. How did she die?"

"I'm really not at liberty to tell you anything more right now." Grayson's forehead wrinkled as his features turned hard as granite. "If it is Helen, Betty will have to make an official identification." He sighed. "But I suspect you're right about the woman's identity."

"I understand." A hundred questions tumbled through Shannon's head.

Sirens sounded in the distance, and Shannon turned to face Melanie and Michael. A sadness welled up inside her. "Betty is going to need all the support she can get. She's at the booth right now with Kate. Grayson wants her to come in to make an official identification."

Michael's expression filled with compassion. "Do you need me to help with anything?"

"Could you go over to the inn and let Tom know ahead of time, so he doesn't have to hear it from the police? We'll get Betty, take her to make the identification, and then bring her back to the inn."

Michael nodded. "I'll stay with Tom until you get there."

Within minutes, Shannon and Melanie picked up Betty from the booth and gave her the bad news. Kate and Melanie offered to search for Joyce to let her know what had happened.

"I'll drive you over to the morgue," Shannon offered.

Betty seemed emotionless, almost numb as she sat next to Shannon in the car. They soon arrived at the morgue, located next to the police station. Shannon parked the car, but Betty made no move to get out. She stared straight ahead, her fingers laced together over her lap.

"I can go in with you if you like."

Betty nodded. "That would be good."

Grayson was waiting for them in the entryway. He led them down a long sterile hallway where the coroner had covered the body with a sheet. He lifted the sheet when Betty stepped closer. Betty looked for a moment as her face drained of all color. "That's her. That's my sister, Helen."

Grayson glanced at the coroner. "I'm sorry to have to be the one to tell you this, but the initial exam suggests someone strangled her."

Murder. The temperature in the already-chilly room room seemed to drop ten degrees.

Betty let out an anguished cry. "I hadn't seen her for forty-five years! And now she's been taken from me again, so quickly. None of this makes any sense!"

Grayson lifted his head. "Forty-five years? People can change a lot in that amount of time."

"Maybe so," said Betty. "But Helen's memories of our childhood were as fresh as if they'd happened only yesterday."

Grayson pulled a notebook out of his back pocket. "Just for record, I need Helen's full name."

"She said she married a man with a last name of Standish. But her maiden name—our name—was Cline." Betty swayed as though her legs might give out on her.

Shannon wrapped her fingers around Betty's upper arm to steady her. "Chief, if it's all right, I'd like to take Betty home now."

Grayson nodded.

Shannon led Betty down what felt like the longest corridor in the world and out into the parking lot. Silence fell between the two women as Shannon drove to the inn. When she pulled into the inn's parking lot, she saw Tom standing in the drive. He took his wife into an embrace and then looked at Shannon. "Would you like to come in? I'm sure she needs her closest friends around at a time like this."

In the living room, Tom brought Betty a hot cup of tea. Shannon sat next to her, holding her hand. Betty shed only a few tears.

Tom settled into a chair opposite Betty. The usually jovial man looked as though he'd been run through a shredder. The doorbell rang, and Joyce, Melanie, and Kate joined the somber group.

The Purls gathered around Betty. Melanie rubbed her back. Instead of peppering Betty with clichés which offered no comfort, all of them allowed for the silent support which would help Betty get through her grief, giving her space to think, cry, and talk—if she needed to.

Finally, Betty spoke up, dabbing at her eyes. "You know what the hardest thing is?"

Shannon squeezed Betty's hand.

"We had such a short time together." Betty twisted a handkerchief in her hands. "I regret that I spent part of our time together being angry at her for not finding me sooner."

"You can't beat yourself up like that," Melanie insisted.

They spent the afternoon together, bringing Betty cups of tea and offering her hugs. Eventually, Kate, Joyce, and Melanie had to leave. A bell rang in the kitchen, indicating a guest was at the check-in counter.

Tom rose to his feet. "I'll take care of that." He touched his wife's shoulder on the way out.

With only Shannon and Betty left in the room, the ticking of the wall clock grew louder. Now that she was alone with Betty, Shannon realized she hadn't seen Michael, though Tom had said he'd been there. He must have slipped out quietly.

Betty sniffled. "I guess life goes on, huh?" Her eyes were red from crying.

Shannon patted her friend's hand. "This will get easier."

The phone rang.

Betty put her face in her hands. "Please—I can't talk to anyone. Not yet."

Shannon let the answering machine pick up the call. It was one of Betty's friends calling to say how sorry she was about her sister.

"How does she already know?" Betty asked.

"Maybe the best thing would be for you to try to lie down," Shannon said.

Betty patted her chest and closed her eyes. "I don't know if I can sleep."

"All of this has been a shock. Rest would do you good. Even if you just lie down on the couch and close your eyes."

"Will you stay with me until Tom gets back?" Betty's expression communicated a level of desperation.

"Of course." Shannon moved to the chair opposite the sofa.

Betty drew her legs up on the couch and closed her eyes. In less than twenty minutes, her breathing became heavier. Shannon grabbed a throw from the back of a chair and gently placed it over her friend.

As she watched Betty sleep, she thought about the circumstances of Helen's death. If Helen had been strangled, had it been with the scarf they had found in the woods? The edge of the park seemed to hold some importance for Helen. She'd been waiting there for someone the day Shannon had shouted her name, and Helen had ignored her. Maybe the road on the other side of the wild orchard was a designated meeting place between her and ... someone.

If Helen died out there, that meant the killer had moved the body. Shannon decided she'd have to give the scarf to Grayson. Feeling her own eyelids growing heavy, she rested her head against the back of the chair.

She awoke when Tom shook her shoulder.

"Sorry it took me so long. The guests need one thing after another, and before you know it, an hour has passed." He turned toward his sleeping wife. "How's she doing?"

Shannon rose from the chair and gestured that maybe they should talk in the kitchen so as not to wake Betty.

Tom followed her. "So how is she?"

"She's holding it together, but ..." Shannon placed her palms on the kitchen counter to steady herself. "This is a lot to deal with."

"Tell me about it." Tom shook his head in disbelief. He wandered around the kitchen, looked out a window, and opened the refrigerator, still shaking his head. He pulled a covered dish out and set it on the counter. "You must be starving. Why don't I heat up some lasagna?"

Shannon knew Tom's coping mechanism was to do what

made him happiest—feed and serve people. "That sounds really good. I'd like that." She hadn't eaten since her early morning breakfast. An applesauce Popsicle hardly qualified as lunch.

"I'm going to have to help with the lunch cleanup in the tearoom. Do you mind staying with her a while longer?" He placed a generous portion of lasagna on a dish and put it in the microwave. "I don't think she should be alone."

"Sure, I can stay," Shannon said.

The microwave dinged, and he pulled out the dish, added a sprig of parsley from an herb garden on the windowsill, and grabbed a napkin from a drawer. "I can pour you some lemonade if you like."

"Thanks, Tom. This is very gourmet."

"If you want, you can sit out on the patio and catch your breath. You can keep an eye on Betty through the patio doors."

"I might just do that." Shannon took her plate and her glass of lemonade and headed outside. From the private patio, she could see the back side of the guest rooms. Some of the curtains were drawn and others remained open. She saw no sign of activity in any of the rooms. By this time of the day, most of the guests were probably headed downtown to shop and enjoy the last full day of the festival.

Shannon took a bite of her lasagna, enjoying the tang of Italian spices on her tongue. As she lifted her glass to sip her lemonade, a scream came from one of the open windows of a guest room.

— 12 —

Shannon bolted to her feet. Within seconds of hearing the scream, she saw a hand push a screen out of a second-story window, a leg appear, and then an entire body emerge as a man dropped to the ground. He bolted for the trees behind the inn. The man wore dark clothes and a hat, but Shannon was pretty sure she knew who he was.

"Stop!" she yelled, chasing after him.

The man favored one of his legs. He must have twisted his ankle when he landed from the second-story window. Due to his limp, Shannon caught up with him easily. She grabbed his shoulders and used her momentum to take him to the ground.

She yanked off his hat and revealed dark, curly hair. "Thought you'd come back for a second time, huh?"

"You again," the man groaned as Shannon placed her knee on his back.

Several people, including Tom, ran from the inn to help her hold the squirming man down.

Shannon shouted, "Call Grayson! I've caught the thief." She turned back to the would-be robber. "Now why don't you tell me why you've targeted the inn?"

The man's voice was strained from the weight of Shannon's knee on his back. "Robbing the guests, what do you think?"

"What were you doing in the office then?"

The thief took a long moment to respond. "I didn't know the layout of the place at first. I was looking for guest rooms. I ended up in the office and decided to look for something of value, so it wasn't a total waste." The man spoke through gritted teeth.

His story didn't ring true—especially if he was the guy who'd tried to run her off the road. He had to be after more than the baubles he could steal from guests.

A plus-size woman dressed in bright colors with hair several different shades of blond hurried toward them. "He was in my room! I came back from shopping because I realized I had forgotten my pocketbook, and there he was."

Even if the thief thought the inn would be mostly abandoned due to the festival, his actions seemed foolhardy. The inn was bristling with people and activity. Why not rob houses where he knew people were out for the day? Either he was the world's stupidest burglar, or something about his story wasn't true.

"What can you tell me about a woman named Helen Standish?" Shannon asked.

Before the thief could answer, Grayson and an officer arrived. After the officer cuffed the robber and led him away, Shannon approached Grayson. "You might want to question him."

"We always do." Grayson's response was terse.

Shannon bit her lower lip. She hadn't meant to sound like she was telling him how to do his job. "Can you find out if he owns a black SUV? I think he might be the person who tried to run me off the road."

"We located that vehicle abandoned outside of town. It was reported stolen a week ago. Wiped down, no fingerprints," Grayson said.

"I'm sure he's the one who tried to run me off the road. Who else could it be?"

Grayson crossed his arms over his chest and furled his brow. "Seems like an extreme response. We don't have anything to link those incidents—or the previous burglary attempt to this one. It's going to be hard to keep this guy in jail, unfortunately."

Shannon took in a breath. "Are you serious?"

"You said you remembered the way the thief smelled that day in the office, not what he looked like."

"But then a man wearing the exact same cologne—this man—ran away from me when I saw him at the parade." Her voice cracked. After all that effort, the guy might walk.

Grayson rubbed his chin. "I know it makes him look guilty, but it's still circumstantial."

Feeling defeated for all her effort, Shannon let out a heavy breath. "So you won't be able to charge him with anything?"

Grayson softened his tone. "He may have taken something from the woman's room just now. If so, we could make that stick. If not, he was in a room that wasn't his own. We can get him for breaking and entering."

Shannon pushed down her rising frustration. "This is the same guy who was in Betty's office the other day. I know it. And I'm positive he's the same guy who kicked me in the head on that fire escape the day of the parade. I saw him—I can identify him. You can at least charge him with that, can't you?"

Grayson's mouth twitched, his version of a smile. "That

one we could charge him with. It won't keep him in jail long though, and bail will be low, if any. "

Shannon pointed out the woman in the bright colors. "She's the woman who found him in her room."

"I'll go have a talk with her." Grayson strode over to the large woman.

Shannon walked slowly back to the patio where her now-cold lunch sat. Worn out from her pursuit, she slumped down at the outdoor table.

Betty opened the sliding glass door. She'd put on a hand-knitted sweater to combat the fall chill. "Tom told me you caught the thief."

"Yes, but unless we figure out if he actually took something either time, Grayson doesn't think he can charge him with anything that will stick for long," Shannon said, looking up at her friend. Dark circles had formed under her eyes, and grief made her skin look almost too heavy for her skull. Shannon decided she really didn't need to burden Betty anymore. "Were you able to get any rest?"

Betty nodded. "I'm feeling much better now." She crossed her arms over her chest. "Helen said she had a daughter in England. I need to find a way to contact her and tell her what's happened. Her daughter needs to know. Helen's suitcase is still in the overflow room. I thought there might be contact information in there. It seems like now it would be OK to look through it … since she's not coming back."

"I'll go with you, and we'll look together."

Leaving the private residence, they walked past the tearoom, where a few people were still eating while the staff cleared the other tables.

"I shouldn't have left Tom so shorthanded," Betty said. "It really takes the two of us plus the staff to run a meal."

Shannon peered into the tearoom. Tom visited and laughed with guests. "I'd say he has everything under control. He understands that you need some time to recover."

Together they climbed the stairs. On the second floor, the large blond woman dressed in bright colors stood in the hallway with her key in the door. Recognition spread across her face when she saw Shannon. "You're the lady who caught the thief just now." She waved her key. "I'm not going to forget to lock this ever again."

"Did the man take anything while he was in your room?" Even though she knew Grayson would do a thorough job investigating, Shannon couldn't resist asking the question. She'd feel safer knowing whether the man could be charged with something that would keep him in jail for awhile.

The woman ran her fingers through her blond hair. "The policeman asked me that too. I don't think he stole anything. I glanced real quickly before I ran out to where you caught him." She turned the key and pushed open the door. "I'm going to look a little closer now."

Shannon stepped forward. "Would you mind if we come in with you?"

"Sure, fine with me." The woman slipped inside and circled the room, turning her head slowly. She opened several drawers and then stood up, placing her hands on her hips. "The thing is, when I came in the room, he was standing there looking around like he had stepped inside only a moment before. Then I screamed, and he ran for the window."

Shannon fought off the sense of despair. "You're positive he didn't take anything?"

The woman glanced around the room one more time. "My pocketbook was right where I left it, out here in the open."

It sounded more like the man was hiding rather than trying to steal something. "Was there anybody else in the hall when you came up here?"

The woman thought for a moment. "Yes. Mr. Russo passed me going the opposite direction. He was carrying a tray of food."

Shannon turned to Betty. "So seeing Tom might have scared the thief, and he hid in the room."

"I wonder where he was really going then," Betty said.

"So do I."

Shannon thanked the woman, and she and Betty stepped out into the hall. Betty opened the door to the overflow room, located next to the woman's room. It was a small space with only a twin bed, small dresser, and no windows or bathroom. Helen's suitcase rested on the end of the bed.

"I wish I could have given her a truly nice room. We don't really have space in our tiny living quarters for guests. I've always put my friends up in a guest room when they come to visit." Betty unzipped the suitcase. "She could have come for a visit in the off-season and would have had the run of the place." She flung open the suitcase. "Now that's not going to happen."

Shannon leaned over to peer inside. The suitcase contained clothing and several pairs of shoes, but no items of a personal nature. Nothing.

"How strange," Betty said, shaking her head. "This could be anybody's suitcase. She hasn't even labeled it with her name."

Shannon agreed. It did seem odd that not a single item connected the suitcase to Helen. "We'll have to ask the chief if they found her purse with her."

"It may have gotten lost in the woods like the scarf did," Betty said.

"Maybe." Shannon didn't want to think about what might have happened in the woods.

Betty unzipped one of the pockets on the suitcase and pulled out a tiny notebook. She flipped through it.

Shannon peered over Betty's shoulder. "Anything?"

"Some really strange notes." She handed the notebook to Shannon.

Shannon read aloud, "Mr. G. dog named Freckles. H likes color periwinkle. Q maiden name Larson."

Shannon held up the notebook. "Who might these people be?"

Betty shook her head and said, "G and H are such common letters. But there was a Quayle staying here for the workshops."

An idea percolated in Shannon's head. "Did Helen spend a lot of time with the guests?"

"Oh yes, she related to the guests really well. She even offered to help out in the tearoom with the serving; she loved talking with them. I really got the impression she wanted to make things easier for Tom and me since her visit came at such a hectic time. That's why I thought it was so strange she didn't want to teach the quilting class, which would have been the biggest help and a better use of her talent."

"Interesting." Shannon wasn't sure about her hunch, but she had a pretty good idea who might be able to help her. "Betty, are you feeling well enough to be alone?"

Betty nodded. "I'll be all right. I might help Tom with the cleanup. Work will get my mind off of things." She leaned a little closer to her friend. "What are you thinking?"

"Not sure yet. I need to check something." Shannon moved toward the door. "I'll call you later."

Shannon headed downtown toward Michael's office. As she got closer to Main Street, she saw a line forming outside the bookstore. She'd forgotten Angel Lewis's book signing happened today. Most of the people standing in line looked like they were under twenty years of age. When she peered into the store window, she saw Angel Lewis perched on a platform, talking into a microphone. The singer's pink and green hair extensions matched her wild outfit.

Shannon smiled. *She looks like one of the cupcakes Joyce makes.*

Angel used big gestures as she talked. Such a contrast from the quiet woman Shannon had met at the park a few days ago.

Shannon looked around for Michael. Though she found plenty of his employees, she couldn't find him. When she looked down the alley by the bookstore, she saw Dylan Manion talking on his cellphone. *Isn't he supposed to be doing security for Angel?*

"We can't be certain about anything until I've looked under every rock," he said. He turned suddenly and saw Shannon. "Gotta go." He clicked his phone shut.

Shannon didn't know what to make of Dylan's cryptic conversation. "I'm looking for Michael."

"I think he's back at the office." Dylan shifted his weight nervously from one leg to the other.

Why is it every time I run into Dylan, he acts like he's hiding something?

"Thanks." Shannon walked around the block and checked in at the store to make sure Essie was still doing OK. Kristin had shown up and was helping the customers. Satisfied the store was in capable hands, she headed down the street to the office of Stone & McCrary. Like Dylan had said, she found Michael in his office, staring at the computer screen with a concerned look on his face.

He lifted his eyes from the computer monitor. "Shannon, it's good to see you. How's Betty doing?"

"Better. It's been one blow after another. It looks like Helen was murdered."

Michael nodded solemnly. "That's got to be rough for Betty."

Shannon pointed toward the computer monitor that had Michael so stressed out. "What are you working on?"

"Our client, Angel Lewis. Her deposit check bounced."

"Really?" Shannon asked. "I would have thought she was rolling in the dough."

"Her credit checked out when I took her on as a client. She said she had an unexpected drain on her account. Sometimes these celebrities aren't real careful how they spend their money." Michael clicked a few keys on his keyboard. "But I'm guessing you didn't stop by to talk about my deadbeat clients."

"Actually, I need to run something by you." She put the notebook Betty had found in Helen's suitcase in front of Michael. "I didn't want to say anything to Betty, because what I'm thinking is really terrible, and I could be wrong. In fact, I'm hoping I'm wrong."

Michael flipped through the notebook. "These look like notes connected with someone speculating about possible computer passwords. People frequently use pets' names and maiden names."

A chill skittered over Shannon's skin even though the office was warm. "That's what I was afraid of. This came from Helen's suitcase. Betty said Helen spent a lot of time talking to the guests under the guise of wanting to help. But then she blew up when Betty suggested the best way she could help would be to teach a quilting workshop since Helen is assumed to be a very talented quilter."

Michael pushed his chair back from his desk. "So, you think Helen was trying to get guests' possible passwords so she could access online information and accounts."

Shannon nodded. "It's a terrible thing to think about a friend's sister. But the more responsibility Helen took on, the more information about the guests she'd have access to. She could learn their home addresses from the guest register. Betty probably would've eventually trusted her enough to let her run credit cards."

Michael held up the notebook. "And she recorded potential password information." He sat back in his chair and pressed his fingers together. "The guests would return home, Helen could use the information for online theft, and it would take months before it was traced back to the inn."

"Even then, Betty and Tom would be the prime suspects."
Shannon got a sick feeling in her stomach. "Do you have a
way to check to see what someone's criminal background is?"

"Of course. I do background checks all the time." Michael
sat up straight in his chair and rolled it toward his desk.

Shannon scooted around to face Michael's computer
monitor. "Betty said Helen's married name was Standish."

Michael typed in a URL and then Helen's full name. He
shook his head. "Nothing."

If she had a grown daughter in England, Helen would
have been married at least twenty years earlier. "Maybe her
criminal record was before she got married," Shannon said.
"Her maiden name is Cline."

Michael tapped the keyboard. A page came up on the
screen that showed a picture of a much younger Helen and
a list of the charges against her, which went back forty years
and stopped five years ago, all under the name of Cline.

"Why would she lie about being married?" Shannon asked.
"Do you suppose she lied about the daughter in England too?"

Michael shrugged and read the screen. "Looks like a lot
of petty stuff—shoplifting, forgery." Michael leaned a little
closer to the screen.

"What is it?"

"A criminal record always list any scars or tattoos a
person might have—anything that would identify them." He
pointed to a line on the screen. "It says here Helen Cline
had a pronounced white scar from her lip to her ear."

Shannon's mouth went dry as shockwaves coursed
through her. "It would be next to impossible to conceal
something like that with makeup." Shannon stood up

straight. "I think I know now why she didn't want to teach the quilting class. She didn't know how to quilt because—"

Michael completed her sentence for her. "Because she wasn't really Helen."

— 13 —

Shannon felt as though she'd been punched in the stomach. "We'd better make sure we're right about Helen before we tell Betty. That poor woman has been through enough."

"I should give Grayson a call and let him know what we've found out." Michael grabbed his cellphone off his desk. Understandably, Grayson had been tight-lipped around Shannon, but he was generally more open with Michael since he had once been a police detective.

Michael dialed the police station and asked for the chief. He quickly explained about the discovery of the notebook and what he'd found online. The rest of the one-sided conversation consisted of Michael nodding and saying "I see" several times.

He hung up.

Shannon leaned in. "Well?"

"They'll take fingerprints from the body. He's going to put a rush on getting a match," Michael said.

"Her purse wasn't with her suitcase. She must have taken it with her to the park. It might contain her real identification. Did Grayson say anything about finding it with the body?"

Michael shook his head. "She had no purse with her or ID." Michael swung his chair around to look at Shannon, offering her a crooked grin. "You've been keeping Grayson pretty busy."

"You mean chasing after the thief at the inn?"

Michael nodded. "Grayson's got his hands full trying to get a warrant to search the man's room down at the Rainbow Motel. We'll see if he has any stolen items stashed there. Otherwise, the only thing he can charge Jason Lynch with is giving you the boot."

"So that's his name—Jason Lynch." Shannon gritted her teeth, her irritation rising about the whole situation. "For being such an inept thief, he sure catches a lot of breaks. They can't tie him to the first break-in because I can't identify him from that. The second time he didn't take anything."

"Chances are they won't set bail very high if that's the case."

"It's so frustrating." Shannon didn't want to think about Jason getting away with a slap to his wrist—and then being free to come after her again. She stared at the information on Michael's computer screen. She wished she could keep her suspicions about Helen's potential theft to herself. Why have Betty go through any more hurt? But if there was a chance Helen had managed to secure sensitive customer information before she died—a chance she'd passed it on to someone else who still intended to use it—Betty and Tom needed to know. And if Helen *was* an imposter, Betty certainly deserved to know that too. "So now we wait to hear from Grayson on both accounts."

"Right." Michael stood up and grabbed a sports jacket off the back of his chair. "I've got to run down to the bookstore, see how things are going. We need to do one more security check before the concert tonight too."

"I suppose I should get back to the store. You'll let me

know as soon as you hear something from Grayson?" she asked, heading toward the door.

"Of course. And Shannon ..."

She turned. "Yes?"

"Be careful. Someone out there didn't want 'Helen' alive. The more questions you ask, the more likely her killer might prefer you were out of the picture too."

Shannon swallowed hard. "I understand. I'll talk to you later." She walked briskly down the street to the Paisley Craft Market, eyeing everyone she passed with renewed suspicion.

Inside the store, Kristin stood by the cash register. Only one customer browsed through the scrapbooking section of the store.

"Been kind of quiet, huh?" Shannon asked.

Kristin nodded. "I think everybody is at the town square or the book signing or saving their energy for the concert tonight."

"Where's Essie?"

Kristin smoothed over her apron. "Making drinks for a couple of people at the coffee bar."

An idea took root in Shannon's mind. "Why don't we close the store a little early?" There might be a way she could get a look at what was in Jason Lynch's motel room without a warrant, but she needed to act on her idea quickly. "I'll total out the day's receipts. That will give you and Essie a chance to have fun at the festival. You might even be able to make the book signing."

A look of terror flashed across Kristin's face, and then she recovered by presenting a stiff smile. "I can total out the receipts."

Shannon had experienced enough drama for one week.

She didn't have the energy to deal with Kristin's strange behavior anymore. She needed to get to the bottom of what was going on. "Kristin, every time I talk about handling the cash drawer, I get a really panicked vibe from you. I've never found any receipt discrepancies. What's going on?"

Kristin stared at the floor and twisted a strand of hair. "I really like this job." Her voice was filled with fear.

"And I like you."

"It would be nice if I could pick up a shift now and then, even after the festival." Kristin still didn't make eye contact.

"You've got to come clean with me. What are you so worried about with this cash register?" Shannon asked the question as gently as she could.

Kristin stared at the ceiling. "It's my mom. She shoplifts. Just small things. It's like she can't help herself."

"Was your mom the one who took some money from the cheerleaders' fundraising box?"

Kristin's eyes widened, and then she slowly nodded. "I've been putting in the dollar amount for what she stole from the store with money from my paycheck, and then I ring it up as a purchase. But they counted the money from the fundraiser before I realized what she had done."

"What your mom does is not right." Shannon couldn't hide her ire. Kristin was a good kid, and this was unfair to her.

Kristin grabbed Shannon's arm. "Please don't turn her in. I might have to go live with my dad, and that would be even worse."

"There has to be some accountability, or she'll keep doing it," Shannon said. "It's not right that you have to cover her tracks. She needs to pay you back, and she needs to get help. I could have a talk with her if you like."

Kristin's eyes glistened with tears. "You would do that for me?"

"Sure I would." Shannon lifted Kristin's chin so she could look the girl in the eye. "I see how hard you work. That counts for something. Now, let's get this place locked up so we can have a little bit of fun."

Essie finished up with the customers in the coffee shop while Kristin helped Shannon close down the store. Shannon flipped the sign from "Open" to "Closed." She checked her phone, hoping maybe she'd missed a text from Michael about the real identity of the woman they had called Helen.

Nothing.

Shannon got in her borrowed car and drove through downtown. She couldn't make the fingerprint match on Helen come back any faster, but she might be able to help in finding some evidence to keep Jason Lynch in jail—a top priority since last night he'd seemed intent on killing her. Grayson needed a warrant to search Jason's motel room, but she didn't. All she needed was a good story.

She knew enough about the law to know that no formal charges could be made unless police gathered evidence after a warrant was in place. But maybe she could find something which would help Grayson come up with an excuse to hold Jason a little longer until the official paperwork came through.

The Rainbow Motel was an older motel on the out-skirts of Apple Grove. All ten of the rooms faced a central courtyard in a horseshoe shape. As she pulled up to the office, dried leaves blew across the concrete.

Inside the office, a girl who looked like she wasn't yet out of junior high school stood behind the counter, a teen magazine open in front of her. She'd pulled her mousy brown hair back with two barrettes, one at each temple. The girl gazed out at Shannon from behind plastic-rim glasses.

Shannon squared her shoulders and spoke with confidence, assuming the girl's parents probably owned the motel. "Hi, my nephew Jason Lynch is staying here."

The girl shifted her weight from one foot to the other and flipped through the magazine, barely looking up at Shannon. "I know Jason. He's been here almost a week."

"Yes, well, unfortunately, he probably won't be coming back here tonight. He's in the Apple Grove jail." Shannon adjusted the shoulder strap of her purse, gauging the girl's reaction.

As she lifted her head, the girl's features compressed, and the furrow between her eyes intensified. "Oh, that's a surprise. He seemed like a nice man. What did he do?"

"They say he broke into a woman's room at The Apple Grove Inn and ransacked the business office," Shannon said.

Shock spread across the teen's face. "Gosh, I had no idea."

"Jason asked if I would bring his toothbrush and some toiletries down to the jail for him. If you could let me in his room ..."

The girl flipped through her magazine, considering. "I suppose that would be OK. But I have to stand and watch you. My mom said I should always do that."

"I understand."

The girl led her to a room on the end of the horseshoe.

She slid a key in and opened the door. A suitcase lay open on the bed. Shannon glanced around the room. A luxury car magazine rested on a chair, and empty fast-food containers cluttered the table. The clothes in his suitcase were neatly folded. There was nothing to indicate Jason had gone on a burglary spree.

Why would a man break into a place twice and not take a single thing?

The girl stood in the doorway. "I bet what you need is in the bathroom."

Shannon headed to the bathroom with the girl on her heels. The only personal items in the bathroom were a comb, toothbrush and a large bottle of cologne. She grabbed the toothbrush, taking the opportunity to glance around. No stolen items anywhere.

Clutching the toothbrush, she returned to the sleeping area of the room. "Actually, I think he keeps his shaving kit in here." She pointed to the suitcase. Carefully, she laid the clothes to one side. Underneath she found two black-and-white photographs. The first one was of a young girl holding a baby. The second was of a couple standing by a car. Shannon flipped the second photograph over. In spidery handwriting, it read, "Mom and Dad with their old Pontiac." Shannon's breath caught. She flipped over the first photo. The handwriting was different. "Helen with baby Eliza."

Shannon struggled to get a deep breath. Just like she'd thought, Jason and the fake Helen had been working this scam together. She didn't need fingerprint results to know she was dealing with an imposter. This wasn't about stealing a little jewelry or money. With all the personal information they intended to have access to at the inn, they were after much bigger fish.

"Did you find what you were looking for?" The young girl's voice held a suspicious note.

Shannon gripped the photos. If she had a chance to dig further in the suitcase, she'd probably find more personal items which aided the imposter in playing the role of Helen and maybe even more evidence of mass identity theft.

Shannon tossed the pictures in the suitcase and hurriedly replaced the clothes. She left the toothbrush on the bed. "He can live without his shaving kit. I don't care anymore."

She jogged to her car, thoughts racing. Jason had broken into the office side of the inn in search of personal information about Betty—things only a sister would know. He must have come back a second time to get the woman's suitcase, fearing it might have information in it which would give them away. Maybe he even thought he'd find her purse there.

Shannon pulled out onto the road and headed back toward town. Still none of what she knew explained why the fake Helen had been killed.

Suddenly, Shannon recalled the conversation she'd overheard outside the inn when "Helen" was on her cellphone. *What if Helen got cold feet and Jason killed her?* Maybe she'd started to feel guilty. Was that why she'd said it was "all too much"? Betty had welcomed her into her life. Maybe the woman—whatever her real name was—had threatened to come clean about their scam, and Jason had gone into a rage and killed her.

Shannon had to make sure the police didn't let Jason go. She called Grayson's direct line but got no answer. She drove straight to the police station. When she stepped inside, Grayson entered the main room from a far door. He sat behind his desk, a pile of papers in front of him. The sagginess of his skin and the dullness in his eyes indicated how long of a day it had been for him.

He lifted his coffee cup and took a sip, glancing up as she approached. "What brings you here, Shannon?"

"You haven't let Jason Lynch go, have you?"

Grayson rolled his chair back. "I'm doing my best to keep him in jail until we can get that warrant. But the assault charges might not be enough. You didn't file a report at the time of the incident."

Shannon tamped down the rising fear. "You have to keep him in custody."

"We're doing everything we can," Grayson said. "But I can't make any promises at this point."

"OK." Shannon took a deep breath. "I understand what you're saying. Has there been any news as to the real identity of the woman who was strangled?"

The chief looked at her for a long moment as the furrows in his forehead deepened. He had never appreciated her and the other Purls "helping" with official police investigations. Maybe she had overstepped her bounds.

"I don't mean to push, Chief," she said. "My main reason for wanting to know is because of Betty."

Grayson slowly nodded. He leafed through the stack of papers in front of him. "Her name is Marilyn Seagrave. She was in the system. Shoplifting. Writing bad checks. And one attempted robbery."

This is all going to be so hard for Betty. Shannon sat down opposite Grayson, propping her purse on her knees and trying to figure out the best way to tell Grayson what she knew about the connection between Jason and Marilyn. She hadn't done anything illegal. She'd been given permission to go in the hotel room … under a false pretense. But Grayson wouldn't be able to put any kind of chain of evidence together until he had the warrant.

Grayson took his fingers off his keyboard. "What is it?"

Shannon bit her lower lip. "I think you should ask Jason Lynch about his connection to Marilyn Seagrave."

Grayson narrowed his eyes as suspicion colored his voice. "Because?"

"I have reason to believe they were working together to rob the guests who stayed at the inn. It appears they were gathering information on the guests. Maybe to go to their houses and rob them, or maybe to use the information to steal from them online, or to commit some sort of identity theft. I don't know." Shannon explained about the notebook she'd found in Marilyn's suitcase and then, a bit more hesitantly, about what she'd found in Jason's motel room.

Grayson raised his eyebrows in response to Shannon's confession. "Makes sense," he said. "Marilyn wins Betty's trust by pretending to be her long-lost sister, which gives her access to all kinds of information."

Shannon was grateful he hadn't made a big deal out of her little bit of independent investigation. "None of it explains why Marilyn was killed or who killed her. Jason *must* know something though. Isn't he the most likely suspect?"

Grayson didn't respond. He took another sip of his coffee, seemingly lost in thought. "I can hold him for

questioning and ... work on making what you found in
the motel room be something which could stand up in
court. Beyond that, I can't make any promises. We may
have to cut him loose soon."

The memory of Jason's anger toward her burned in her
mind. She really didn't want him back out on the street,
looking for her. "I want to be the one to tell Betty about
Marilyn. I'd rather she hear it from a friend."

"Me too," said Grayson.

Shannon exited the building and hurried to Deborah's
car. Her phone rang as she stuck the key in the ignition.

"Hey, honey." Even through the phone, her mom's voice
transmitted warmth.

"Hi, Beth. How are things at the park?"

"Still pretty busy. You haven't been by all day today,
and no one is at the Purls booth. One of your friends came
by a while ago and packed everything up." Beth hesitated.
"I wondered what was going on."

Shannon gave her mother the short version of everything that had happened. "I'm headed up to Betty's to break
the news to her right now."

"Were you planning on coming to the concert? I was
hoping to see you, but I'll understand if you can't. You've got
a lot on your plate."

"I'm not sure. Are you ... leaving town?" Shannon's
voice faltered, giving away her disappointment.

"One of the Gourmet on the Go trucks in Portland is
having issues that my employees can't seem to handle. I
need to leave as soon as the concert is over with."

"I'm really going to miss having you here." Shannon's

sentiment came out so naturally. "I hope we can get together again soon, during a time when things aren't so busy."

"I'd like that."

"I will try to get over to the concert before you leave." Shannon said goodbye and pulled out of the police station lot. A tight knot formed in her stomach as she turned onto Meadowlark Street and approached the inn.

Can Betty handle yet another emotional blow?

— 14 —

Shannon parked and entered The Apple Grove Inn through the main lobby. No one greeted her from behind the front desk. She poked her head into the tearoom, which was empty of patrons since they didn't serve dinner. There was no sign of Tom or Betty either.

She walked to the private residence side of the inn and knocked on the door. Nobody answered. She'd just about decided to give up looking for them when she heard laughter coming from the patio. Shannon circled around to the side of the house.

Melanie and Joyce sat with Betty, eating pastries and sipping mugs of steaming liquid. Shannon breathed a sigh of relief. *Why did I think I had to be a support to Betty alone?* She had some of the best friends in the world. They knew Betty would need some extra encouragement.

Joyce pushed back her chair and winked at Shannon. "Good to see you, stranger."

Melanie turned. "What have you been up to, Shannon?" She clearly had no idea what a loaded question she'd asked.

"We're all thinking of going to the concert together," Joyce said, twirling her finger around the rim of her mug.

"The girls have talked me into it," said Betty.

"We think it's better if she doesn't isolate herself or bury herself in work," Melanie added. "That's not healthy after all she's been through."

The knot in Shannon's stomach tightened. And here she was about to dump more bad news on Betty. "Going to the concert together sounds like a great idea." Her attempt at cheerfulness fell flat. She wished she could attend the concert and forget everything she had discovered, but she wanted to get to the bottom of all of it for Betty.

"Seriously, Shannon. What's on your mind?" Melanie took a bite of her pastry.

"It's a long story and not a happy one." Shannon looked at Betty.

Melanie rose to her feet and pulled out a chair for Shannon. "We're all here but Kate. We can handle it together."

"I'll be all right, no matter what the news is," Betty assured. "I've got my friends with me. That's what matters."

Shannon told the Purls everything she'd learned about Jason, and then she informed them that the woman in the morgue was not Helen Cline. She watched Betty's face blanch as she shared the news.

"You're saying the dead woman isn't my sister?" Betty shook her head. "But she looked like her—like I remembered her. She had the same blue eyes."

Betty was remembering things through the lens of an adoring eight-year-old child. Certainly Marilyn Seagrave must have borne a solid resemblance to the real Helen, but after forty-five years, it would have been easy enough to convince anyone.

Shannon settled into a patio chair. "The woman in the morgue is Marilyn Seagrave. Not Helen Cline."

Betty continued to shake her head in disbelief. "But the quilts. Those *were* Helen's quilts. How would this person have gotten them? Somebody else couldn't have made them. I recognized my sister's handiwork—the unique patterns—even after all these years."

"Perhaps she knew Helen," said Melanie. "And she bought the quilts from her, or they were a gift."

"Yeah, or she *stole* the quilts from Helen," Joyce chimed in. "Either Jason or this Marilyn person must have crossed paths with Helen."

"I agree," said Shannon. "They knew about Betty and the inn. That means they had to have known the real Helen at some point. I think the quilts were a very clever way of lending credibility to the ruse that Marilyn was Helen. They were mailed ahead to prime you to the idea of Helen showing up after all these years."

"But how did my sister even know I ran an inn?" Betty's eyes brightened, and the corners of her mouth curved up. "She must have been trying to find out about me. That means Helen—the *real* Helen—is still out there somewhere."

Shannon left out the details about Helen's police record, which ended five years ago. She wanted to spare Betty any more pain than necessary. Shannon wasn't so sure Betty should get her hopes up about having a reunion with her sister. If the real Helen *had* been looking for Betty, what had kept her from making contact? It was possible that Jason and Marilyn did something to prevent Helen from making contact with her sister—ever. If the real Helen showed up, their scam would be ruined.

"I wonder what she's been doing." Betty couldn't hide the excitement in her voice. "She must have children and grandchildren."

"What an amazing turnaround! She might be out there somewhere trying to find you." Melanie sounded almost as joyous as Betty.

Shannon wasn't so sure they should be heading down that hopeful path yet.

"But then why would she find out where Betty lived, that she ran the inn, and then not come to see her?" Joyce's voice held a note of somberness.

Shannon breathed a sigh of relief that Joyce had brought a reality check into the conversation.

Betty slumped back in her seat. "Maybe she can't because Jason and Marilyn did something to her so they could run this scam."

"This is all speculation," said Shannon.

Joyce jumped to her feet. "All this talk is making me sad. This is the last full day of the festival. We should go and have some fun. Who's with me?"

"I am." Melanie scooted her chair back. "A lot of people bring a picnic and eat dinner in the park before the concert starts. What do you say, Betty? Are you ready to decompress for a bit after all the stress you've had this week?"

Betty slowly nodded. "We probably have some leftovers from the tearoom meals. I can throw something together." She pushed back her chair and stood.

"That sounds great. I'll give you a hand. We'll call Kate, and she can meet us there." Joyce turned toward Shannon. "Are you coming?"

"Give me a minute. I need to make a call first."

While the other women bustled inside, Shannon stood

on the patio listening to Michael's phone ring and praying he would pick up.

"Hello, Shannon." His tone was warm and relaxed.

"You must be checking your caller ID."

"Every time."

Shannon turned to face the trees surrounding the back of the inn. "I need your help. Are you still sitting in front of your computer?"

"Yes. You caught me just in time. In another ten minutes, I would have been out the door to the park."

"Could you do something for me?" she asked. "We have a name now for the woman who was pretending to be Helen. Marilyn Seagrave. Would it be possible to cross-reference Marilyn's name with Helen's and see if they were ever in the same prison at the same time?"

"I can do that. It'll take me a minute. I have to pull up both their criminal records and compare." She could hear the sound of fingers tapping a keyboard.

The sliding glass door opened, and Melanie stuck her head out. "We're about ready to leave."

Shannon pulled the phone away from her ear. "I'll catch up with you guys in a minute. I'm driving Deborah's car."

"See you at the park." Melanie slid the door shut.

Michael's voice came across the line. "Shannon?"

"I'm here."

"Both women did time at the same women's prison, but there was no overlap in their sentences."

"That's not what I'd expected you to say." She couldn't hide her disappointment. "Helen must have known Marilyn at some point."

"Maybe Helen confided in Jason about her long-lost sis-ter," Michael said. "That could be the connection."

"That's a possibility. Helen could've met one of them on a bus, or they might have been neighbors. Marilyn surely would have noticed the resemblance between the two of them. But somehow she or Jason acquired Helen's quilts. Betty knew who had made those quilts just by looking at them, and it gave Marilyn enough legitimacy to walk into the Russos' lives."

"It's a lot to unravel," Michael said.

"Thank you for doing this, Michael." Shannon looked at her watch. "I don't want to keep you from your work."

"My men can pretty much run the show without me. I've got a good crew." He paused. "Dylan really stepped up to the plate."

Shannon held her breath. Her impression of Dylan Man-ion was substantially different from the impression Michael held. What if Dylan had completely pulled the wool over his eyes? Maybe Michael had a blind spot because Dylan acted like the son he never had. She owed it to Michael to say something. "I'm glad you're pleased with Dylan. I do have to say that every time I run into him, he acts like he's up to something he shouldn't be. I don't know how to explain it. It could just be my perception, but I thought I should tell you ... as a friend."

A heavy silence fell between them. Shannon feared she'd pushed too far.

"Has he said anything to you to make you feel this way?" Though Michael spoke in a monotone, tension colored each word.

Shannon regretted even bringing it up. "No. It's that he *acts* suspicious."

"I appreciate the feedback, but why don't you let me run my business?"

"Michael, I'm sorry if I offended you but—"

"I need to get over to the park." Michael hung up.

Stunned, Shannon turned off her phone. She tilted her head back and combed her fingers through her thick, wavy hair. Michael had sounded more defensive than she'd ever heard before. *Was I that out of line?*

She put her phone back in her purse and slid the patio door open. When she stepped inside, the quilts caught her eye. Shannon drew one of them out of the box. It was a simple Four-Patch pattern, but the color choice, the blending of prints and solids, revealed that a superb artist had made the blanket. If she could only discover the connection between Marilyn and Helen, she might find out what happened to the real Helen.

She gently placed the quilt back in the box. As she did, one of the corners flipped back. She leaned over to flatten it out. On the back of the quilt, in faint blue letters, were stamped words. Shannon leaned a little closer to read, "Property of Hope House. Seattle, Washington."

Shannon's thoughts kicked into high gear. *Is Hope House the connection between Marilyn and Helen?*

It would be nice to pull out her laptop and do some research on this Hope House. Most places had a website these days. But she'd have to wait. The other Purls were expecting her at the park.

She left the inn and slipped in behind the steering wheel

of Deborah's car. As she put the key into the ignition, she heard sirens sounding through the streets. It didn't sound like the typical lone ambulance. It sounded like an army of them. The noise grew louder and more intense as they approached.

What kind of accident or emergency would cause this level of response?

— 15 —

As the sirens' screams echoed in her ears, Shannon's cell-phone rang, vibrating her purse. Michael's number flashed on the screen.

She half-expected, half-hoped he was calling back to apologize for snapping at her when she'd only been trying to protect him from a bad employee.

"Yes," she answered.

"I heard on the scanner that Jason Lynch had some sort of medical emergency. They're taking him to the hospital now."

Shannon couldn't quite process the information. "That means he's not in jail."

"Yeah, that was my first thought too. Seems kind of fishy."

"We should probably give him the benefit of a doubt."

"No, you should probably be careful since you're not his favorite person," Michael said. Maybe it was because of their previous conversation, but his tone was curt, like he was *ordering* her to be careful. She heard none of the concern he'd shown on earlier occasions.

"I'm going to a concert," she said. "I'll be in a crowd. I'll be fine. Besides, I'm sure Grayson has him in protective custody."

Michael muttered something under his breath that Shannon didn't quite catch. "Fine," he said, his words clipped. "I just called to let you know." He hung up on her. Again.

Shannon stared at the phone. Clearly she'd really upset him when she'd shared her suspicions about Dylan. In the past, he'd also been appreciative—impressed even—of her perceptiveness about people. But not when it came to his choice in personnel.

The sirens died out as she started the car and headed toward downtown. She eased past the hospital where police and ambulance lights flashed.

Even from a distance, she recognized Grayson's form as it disappeared into the emergency room behind a gurney pushed by two EMTs. A second officer lingered in the parking lot, Officer Brownley. Brownley tended to be less tight-lipped than Grayson. Her friends expected her at the concert, but it wouldn't hurt to stop and ask a few quick questions.

Shannon turned the car around and eased into the ER entrance.

Brownley nodded his head in recognition as she approached him. "Shannon, what are you doing here?" His expression turned serious. "You're not hurt, are you?"

She smiled. "No. Michael Stone called me. He said there had been a medical emergency at the jail."

"Jason Lynch never told us he was diabetic." Brownley pushed his hat back and wiped the perspiration from his forehead.

"Oh dear. What happened?"

"He got all shaky and crazy. He didn't tell us what was going on until it was too late." Clearly upset, Brownley took his hat off and twirled it in his hands. "It was his responsibility to inform us he needed his medication. We had no way of knowing."

Brownley was an eager but inexperienced officer in his early twenties. He seemed to be taking the whole thing pretty hard. Shannon spoke in a more soothing tone. "You're right. He should have told you."

"I honestly thought he was losing it because of the questions Grayson had asked him, about his connection to Marilyn Seagrave. Course we couldn't bring up the photos you found in his room. Grayson kind of implied we knew there was a connection without saying how we knew."

"Did Jason admit anything?" Shannon was grateful she'd caught the officer. Grayson probably wouldn't have been as eager to share with her.

"He said he was hired by someone who communicated via text and email. Doesn't know if it was a man or woman."

So there's a third person involved. "He doesn't know anything about why Marilyn was killed?"

Brownley shook his head. "We didn't get that far. I think the interview might have stressed him." The officer balled his hand into a fist and shook his head. "He should have told us. We would have seen to it that he got his medication."

Shannon patted Brownley's arm. "You're not at fault here."

"We would never mistreat a suspect." Brownley's anxiety over the situation caused sharp creases to form around his eyes and mouth.

"I know you wouldn't," Shannon said. "You guys have always done a great job."

"I better get inside. The chief is going to wonder what happened to me. I've got to watch Lynch until it's OK for him to go back to the jail, *if* he's OK to go back to the jail."

Brownley turned and walked toward the emergency room doors.

Still stirred up over the new development, Shannon returned to the car and drove toward Main Street. She opted to park in front of the now-dark Paisley Craft Market rather than risk not being able to find a space closer to the concert. On a cool fall evening like this, the short walk would be pleasant. She picked up her pace as her thoughts returned to Jason Lynch. He'd been backed into a corner and then had confessed that an anonymous mastermind put him up to the thievery. Was that the truth? Or was it simply his way of trying to get the charges against himself reduced?

"Evening, Mrs. M." Matthew Conlin fell in step beside her.

Startled out of deep thought, Shannon regained her composure. "Hey, Matthew, how is the sculpting business?"

"Not as good as the master welder business. But I did manage to sell a couple of my bigger pieces."

"It's never a bad thing to make a little money doing what you love."

"I was sorry to hear you and your friends weren't able to keep your booth open. I certainly understand the reason," Matthew said, keeping pace beside Shannon as they made their way toward the park. "It's too bad about Betty's sister."

"Yes, it's sad for Betty more than anything." Shannon didn't want to reveal all that she knew about the case, and that the woman that was killed had not been Betty's sister after all.

Shannon and Matthew arrived at the edge of the park, which was already teeming with activity. Even though the rumor mill in Apple Grove was pretty efficient, Grayson seemed to have kept a tight lid on the real identity of the murdered woman. Matthew certainly hadn't heard the whole story.

"Do they know how she died?" he asked.

Shannon cast him a sideways glance. Maybe Matthew was only making conversation. All the same, she didn't feel the need to let any more information leak out than necessary. "The police are still working on it."

Matthew nodded in understanding. He turned slightly, scanning the park. "Your friends are waving at you."

Joyce, Kate, and Melanie were all standing up, doing their impersonation of cheerleaders. Betty sat on the ground beside the picnic basket. She'd brought along an old blanket and laid it on the ground to sit on.

Shannon's friends' silliness lifted her spirits. "They've been waiting for me," she said.

Matthew pointed toward a group of men who looked like they'd come straight from a construction site. Most of them wore plaid shirts and heavy-duty work pants. "There's my party over there. We're looking forward to hearing Angel Lewis."

"The whole town is," Shannon said. "Catch you later." She pushed through the crowd to join her friends.

"What took you so long, kiddo?" Joyce asked.

"A slight delay."

"We waited for you before we ate." Kate dropped down on the edge of the afghan and crossed her legs.

Melanie opened the picnic basket and offered each person a plastic plate. "Are you thinking you might try to find your sister now, Betty?"

Shannon assumed she'd missed out on some part of the conversation by being late.

Betty stared at the ground. "When this imposter died, and I thought I had lost my sister ... well, it made me realize how short our time on this earth is. Before we were married, Tom and I did try to find Helen. We couldn't afford to hire a detective. When there was no trace of her in the area, I assumed she was dead."

Shannon's heart squeezed tight. She'd hoped to spare Betty of the knowledge of her sister's criminal past. If Betty went looking for Helen, she might be in for even more heartache.

The women enjoyed the leftovers while several warm-up acts took the stage. The first was the high school choir, followed by a local band which sang cover tunes.

Melanie took a bite of chicken. "This is fabulous."

"Gertrude does a great job as our cook," Betty said.

"Your mom has fabulous food on her truck too, Shannon. I bought a fish taco the other day from her." Melanie looked up from her plate. "Where is she now? I don't see her."

Shannon glanced over at the line of food vendors. Her mother's truck wasn't there. "I don't know. I was hoping I'd get the chance to say goodbye to her before she left for Portland tonight. But I must have missed her."

Melanie wrapped an arm around Shannon. "Maybe she ran out of food and is going to be back later."

"Oh, look at that." Kate pointed toward the stage where a man was instructing his trained poodles to jump through hoops. "Bill brings Mitzi and Tiffany in all the time for grooming. He said he was going to perform tonight, but I had no idea they were so good."

As they got closer to the time when Angel Lewis would

take the stage, the area around them filled with people sitting in lawn chairs and on blankets.

Both Melanie and Joyce wiggled as they sat.

"My old tush is not designed to sit like this," Joyce commented. "I'll die from the pain before the concert is over."

Shannon sat up on her knees. "I have some stadium chairs back at the shop. I could run and get them."

"Great idea," said Joyce. "I could use a little more cushion and back support."

"Go ahead. It's probably going to be another twenty minutes before Angel takes the stage anyway," Melanie said, gathering up the empty paper plates.

"I'll be back in a flash." Shannon jogged to the shop. The streets were nearly empty—half the town was at the park. Going to the shop gave her the excuse she needed to find out more about Hope House. She let herself in and walked through the darkened store to the coffee shop, which provided a laptop for customers to use for short intervals. She clicked on the single light next to her and turned on the computer. It took her only minutes to find out that Hope House was a halfway house for parolees in Washington state. She found the phone number on the Hope House website and pulled out her cellphone to dial.

"Hello, Hope House, Meredith speaking." The woman's voice sounded upbeat.

"Hi, I'm sorry to bother you late at night."

"It's no bother, dear. We're open 24/7. What can I help you with?"

"I'm trying to locate two people who may have stayed at your place. One of them is named Marilyn Seagrave, and the other may have gone by the name Helen Cline."

Silence.

Shannon pursed her lips. Of course this woman—as nice as she sounded—wasn't going to give out information to a complete stranger without a compelling reason. Perhaps a less blunt tactic would work better. "What I'm most interested in is locating Helen Cline. Her younger sister, Betty, wants to find her. If Helen did stay there, she may have referred to Betty as Eliza. Her sister really wants to get in touch."

"Oh, Helen, sure," Meredith said, her voice taking on a positive tone.

"You remember her then." Shannon's voice filled with excitement.

"Who could forget Helen? She must have made two dozen quilts and gave them to us and anybody who admired them. They were so beautiful. We even used some for our fundraisers."

Shannon didn't quite know how to phrase her next questions. "So she was … nice when she stayed there?"

"Helen reformed her life while she lived here. She'd been in and out of jail from a young age, but by the time my husband and I met her, I could see God had truly transformed her life."

"Do you know what happened to her?"

"She left here at least four or five years ago." Meredith spoke slowly. "It's interesting that her sister is looking for Helen now. Helen talked often about finding her little sister. We even helped her do some of the leg work to locate Eliza."

"But you don't know what happened to her once she left your facility?"

"She didn't stay in touch with us, which is too bad. Such

a sweet woman." Meredith paused, perhaps running memories of Helen through her head. "And what was the other woman's name? Why did you want to know about her?"

Shannon scrambled. She should have thought this through before she dialed the number. "We think Marilyn Seagrave may know of Helen's whereabouts."

"That name is not ringing a bell. I can check our database real quick, if it will help reunite the two sisters." She heard the woman tapping a keyboard. "Ah, yes, she was here about the same time as Helen. I remember now. We called them the twins because they looked so much alike. I really can't say what happened to her once she left here. Quiet woman. Kind of shut down emotionally."

Shannon felt elated. She'd finally found the connection between Helen and Marilyn. "That's all right. You've told me everything I need to know."

"Well, if you do get in touch with Helen, we sure would like to hear from her," Meredith said.

"I'll pass it on." Shannon hung up the phone and shut down the computer. The glow from the monitor faded, and the only illumination in the entire shop was the light above the booth she sat in. Helen had laid the groundwork to find Betty five years ago, but then didn't follow through. Why not? Had something happened to her?

Marilyn must have learned about the inn from Helen. She could have taken the quilts from Hope House, or she could have been given them. Something must have spurred Marilyn to put together the scheme to defraud the guests at the inn, and maybe even Betty and Tom, once she gained their trust and had access to information. Who knew how far she, Jason, and their mastermind partner had planned to take their scam.

A money stream like that would be worth killing for—in some people's eyes. Shannon couldn't clearly say if the person who'd run her off the road was a man or woman. Could it have been the mastermind Jason had referenced? Maybe this third person had the computer savvy to pull off the elaborate theft.

Jason claimed he'd remained in town because he hadn't been paid for his efforts.

Supposing Jason was telling the truth, she would need to find out from him when his last communication with the mastermind had occurred. Had he decided to go back and get Marilyn's suitcase on his own, or had he been ordered?

The chair scraped the floor as she stood up. There were so many questions to sort through. She looked at her watch and rushed to the storage room to grab the stadium chairs.

When she entered the retail area of the shop again, she saw a man standing by the door inside the shop and stifled a gasp.

I'm sure I locked the door behind me.

Heart pounding, she slipped behind a display and waited for him to turn around.

— 16 —

Shannon's throat tightened and a rapid pulse drummed in her ears. She reached into her purse, searching for her cellphone. The unknown man slowly turned around, his brown hair catching the light that spilled in from the street.

Then she saw his face.

Shannon let out a heavy breath and stepped out from behind the display. "Matthew."

Matthew stuttered in his step, and he dropped something onto the floor. "Mrs. M.! You nearly gave me a heart attack."

"I could say the same about you."

He stepped toward her. "What are you doing in here in the dark?"

"I was in a hurry. I didn't want to take the time to turn on the lights." Shannon edged toward the wall, fumbling for the light switch. "What are *you* doing in here?"

"Essie sent me. She said there were some old display quilts we could use to sit on," Matthew said. "The hard ground gets uncomfortable after a while."

"How did you get into the shop?"

Matthew reached down on the floor to retrieve the keys he'd dropped. "She gave me the keys. I hope that's OK."

Shannon wasn't so sure about that. Essie was plenty trustworthy, but it didn't seem like a good idea to let other people have the keys to the store, even Matthew. "So you and Essie are sitting together at the concert."

"Yeah, we sort of met up. She and some of her friends hooked up with me and some of my friends."

"Well, go get the quilts. Give me the keys. I'll make sure they're returned to Essie."

Matthew held the keys protectively to his chest. "Don't you trust me?" He narrowed his eyes at her.

"I don't want the keys getting lost. I think it's better if I keep them." Shannon held out her hand. Matthew dropped the keys into her palm. The tightness in his features told her she'd fractured something in their blossoming friendship. "Forgive me, Matthew, I've had a lot of things happen lately which make me suspicious when I probably shouldn't be."

"Where are those quilts at anyway?" His voice was still a little icy.

"They're behind the counter, folded up." Shannon placed the keys in her purse, wondering what more she could say.

Matthew's cowboy boots pounded across the floor, and then he leaned down behind the counter. He stood up holding three small folded quilts. He looked off to the side and shook his head. "I guess Essie shouldn't be giving out those keys to anybody."

The inflection of his words revealed he was still miffed. She chose to ignore it. "It's a nice night. Let's walk back over to the park together and enjoy the concert." Shannon turned off all the lights, set the alarm, and double-checked to make sure the door locked behind them.

When they returned to the park, clusters of people

talked in huddles, and the lines at the food carts had grown longer. There was still no sign of Beth. The lights dimmed on the empty stage.

Shannon rejoined the Purls, and each of the women eagerly grabbed a stadium chair. "What's going on?" she asked.

"There's been a slight delay in Angel Lewis taking the stage," Joyce explained.

"They're building the suspense." Melanie adjusted her straw hat.

"That man is waving at you." Kate grabbed Shannon's upper arm and pointed off to the side by the food trucks.

Not more than forty yards away stood Hunter Banks. "That's the man who gave Beth and me a ride when we got run off the road. He moved here to do research on fish or something." Shannon waved back.

"He's handsome in a surfer dude sort of way," Melanie said before settling down in her chair.

Kate leaned close to Melanie and looked over her shoulder. "An old surfer dude."

"Old?" Shannon gave Kate's shoulder a friendly pat. "What are you talking about? He's my age." She unfolded her stadium chair next to Melanie.

"That's what I said." Kate laughed.

A cheer rose up from the crowd as the lights over the stage came up, and Angel Lewis's band hustled onto the stage to pick up their instruments. A hush fell across the park. The band began to play the melody of one of Angel's hit songs, and everyone cheered.

Joyce leaned close to Shannon and whispered in her ear

above the noise. "Is Angel ever actually going to perform?"

Shannon shook her head and raised her hands up in an I-don't-know motion. Finally, after an extended instrumental interlude from the band, Angel Lewis stepped up to the microphone. The crowd went wild. Angel's sequined blue dress and hot pink sequined cape glittered beneath the stage lights.

Angel raised her hands. "Good evening, Apple Grove! It's good to be back in a place that means so much to me."

The crowd cheered.

"If you read my book, *Caught in the Whirlwind*, you know I spent my last two years of high school here living with a wonderful family." Angel spoke as the band played softly in the background.

"Good thing she worked in that plug for her book," said Joyce.

"I think she means what she says about Apple Grove," said Shannon. "There are much bigger places where she could have promoted her book."

Angel pulled the microphone off the stand. "Let's get started!" She whirled into motion as the band cranked up the volume.

Angel belted out her first number. Shannon saw Kristin bobbing up and down with the other teenagers toward the front of the stage. Shannon buttoned up her jacket and stood up along with the other Purls, holding out a hand to help Betty to her feet.

They swayed and clapped to the music, turning to each other and laughing from time to time.

"Oh, to be a teenager again!" Joyce exclaimed.

Angel launched into a song with an intense backbeat. The park seemed to grow even more crowded as people squished closer together, dancing and swaying to the music.

Amidst the loud cheering and clapping, Shannon glanced over at Betty. Though she, too, was smiling, the dullness in her eyes hinted at the sadness and confusion she must have been wrestling through. The Purls had made a good call when they talked Betty into attending the concert. If she'd stayed at the inn, she might have been consumed by the strong emotions battling within her.

Tomorrow there would be time for Shannon to get Betty alone and reveal what she'd discovered. And then Betty could decide whether or not to pursue the search for her sister. Had something happened to the real Helen? Shannon didn't know, but she owed it to her friend to share the news that Helen was well thought of when she had left the halfway house five years ago.

Angel switched to a ballad, and most of the audience sat down. The teenagers at the front of the stage continued to sway to the music, but the Purls settled back into their chairs.

"That sounds more like something I listened to when I was in high school." Betty closed her eyes and tilted her head side to side in time to the music.

Shannon glanced around at the crowd. Sissy, Kristin's mom, sat several groups of people away. *Poor Kristin, having to cover up for her mother's criminal compulsion.*

Eventually, Angel sang her final song. Even Shannon recognized the melody of *Whirlwind*. The pop star introduced the members of her band and exited the stage. The crowd close to the stage clapped and called for an encore even while the rest of the crowd packed up their blankets, picnic baskets, and chairs.

Joyce pushed herself to her feet. "I don't know about you guys, but I am ex-haust-ed."

"I know tomorrow's Sunday, but maybe we can all get together after church before the shop opens up at one instead of waiting for our usual time on Monday," Melanie said. She looked directly at Betty when she spoke.

Betty squared her shoulders and lifted her chin. "I'll be there. I know it's important to get out of the house."

The Purls said their goodbyes, offering each other hugs and then going in separate directions. As the mass exodus from the park started, and cars roared to life in the parking lot and on the side streets, Shannon kept her eye on Sissy. The crowd swirled around her, and she felt a little like a fish swimming upstream. She called out to Sissy, but the woman didn't turn around.

Is it even worth it to deal with this now? She'd made a promise to Kristin that she would talk to Sissy about her stealing problem, and she didn't want to break it. With everything else in her life so uncertain, she wanted something to be resolved before the day was over. In Shannon's brief interaction with Sissy, she hadn't seemed like a difficult person. If Shannon could frame the conversation in a kind way, maybe it would lead Sissy to get some counseling for her compulsive stealing.

She pushed through the crowd, spying Sissy at a distance. Sissy's stark white jacket was easy enough to keep track of in the crowd as she headed into the woods at the edge of the park. Shannon followed the path through the trees. She'd lost sight of Sissy but knew the way to her house. Hopefully, she would catch Sissy before the woman went inside. If not, she'd have to let the issue go until another day. It would be rude to knock on Sissy's door at such a late hour.

The noise from the park slowly died away, and Shannon's footsteps stuttered. She'd been so keen to chase down Sissy. Now that she was halfway through the woods, where Marilyn Seagrave may have been abducted or strangled, it occurred to her that it might have been better to wait and talk to Sissy on another day. Especially considering there was a third partner in the scheme against the inn—a person who might know of the trouble she'd caused.

Shannon hurried her steps.

Dry leaves crackled in the wind. Branches creaked. Without a flashlight, the trees created a tunnel effect. She stepped carefully through the thick underbrush.

Maybe the murderer hadn't wanted the body to be found so close to the park because it would place suspicion on him or her. The warehouse might have been the first place that seemed like a safe bet. Melanie had said the doors were not locked. But the killer had to know the body would have been found there eventually.

Shannon stepped out onto the road, relieved to see the porch lights of the little houses. Only Sissy and an older man headed across the road to their homes.

"Sissy!" Shannon called out.

Sissy turned and waved. "Mrs. McClain."

Shannon jogged over to meet Sissy on the road. "I know it's late, but I wanted to talk to you. Do you have a minute?"

"Sure. Why don't we go on inside?" Sissy pointed toward her house.

Shannon expected trepidation or suspicion from Sissy, but she'd seen neither of those in the other woman's reaction. She followed Sissy up the steps. The exterior of the house was cute but in need of a coat of paint.

Sissy unlocked the door and pushed it open. "What is it you wanted to talk to me about?" She walked into the kitchen where the little dog Shannon had seen before greeted her. "Is everything all right with Kristin at the store? She's working hard, isn't she? I told her to give a hundred and ten percent, and you might have some more work for her even after the festival."

Shannon glanced around. The room was clean but sparse, with no mementos or anything that personalized the place other than a few photos of Kristin at various stages of her life scattered haphazardly on a side table. A newer-model laptop sat on a desk in the living room.

"Kristin is doing a great job," Shannon said.

After Sissy put down the dog, he ran over to his food dish.

"I'm glad to hear that." Sissy stared at Shannon for a long moment, as if her mind were sorting through what else Shannon could possibly want to talk about. Certainly, the woman would have some guilt over the position she'd put Kristin in.

The emptiness of the room nagged at Shannon. "How long ago did you and Kristin move here?"

Sissy's spine straightened and her eyes narrowed slightly. "Is that what you came to talk to me about?"

"Actually, no. I wanted to talk about you." Shannon kept her voice level, trying not to sound accusatory.

Sissy's expression hardened. "About me?"

Shannon glanced around the room. It really looked like a house where someone wasn't planning on settling in. She remembered Jason's assertion that he had only been hired help. Shannon glanced around at the furnishings. Everything in the house was old and rundown except for the laptop. Whoever pulled off this scheme would have to know something about computers.

Perspiration formed on Shannon's forehead even as a shiver ran down her back.

"You know, it's getting late." Shannon took a step back. Marilyn had last been seen only yards from where Sissy lived. Sissy had recently moved into town—and she'd demonstrated she was capable of criminal behavior. "I didn't mean to bother you. We can talk another time."

"You came here to tell me something. So tell me." Sissy swiped a plastic cup off the counter and tossed it in the sink. She whirled back around to face Shannon. "Why does it matter to you how long we've lived here?"

Shannon sensed Sissy's anger lying beneath the surface, threatening to erupt.

Without warning, a strong gust of wind buffeted the windows, making them shake. Shannon jumped as the windows continued to rattle. The little dog looked up at her and let out a single sharp bark.

Shannon suddenly felt very vulnerable. "It's late. This isn't going at all how I planned. I really think I should be leaving."

Sissy took a step toward her. "Are you going to tell me why you followed me all the way out here or not?" Her eyes turned hard as granite, and Shannon wondered if she was standing in a room with a killer.

"Like I said, we can deal with it another time." Shannon rushed toward the door. "I really need to go." She pushed open the door and raced outside, hurrying toward the band of trees which led back to the park. When she looked behind her, Sissy stood in the open doorway of the house. Shannon picked up her pace and dashed through the thick underbrush. In the quickly fading light, branches grabbed at her hair and scraped her face, but she didn't care. She ran as fast as she could. As she neared the clearing, she dared to look over her shoulder again, but saw no one. Only the trees met her gaze as they rustled and creaked in the wind.

Finally, she burst from the woods and staggered out onto the open lawn of the park. The place had gone from being the population center of Apple Grove to looking almost completely abandoned. A few stragglers made their way through the park. Some blankets and left-behind empty soda cans littered the grass. Only the stage still looked busy as the roadies tore down the set.

She glanced around, looking for Michael, but saw no sign of him. She needed his help. Shannon pulled out her phone and dialed his number. Would he even talk to her after their spat about Dylan? The phone rang three times and then went to voice mail.

"Hello, Michael. It's me. I'm wondering if you could check into the background of a woman named Sissy O'Connor for me. It's a hunch, but I think she may be connected to Marilyn's death. Sorry to bother you."

Shannon paced as she spoke, drawing nearer to the

stage. Off to one side, Dylan stood close to Angel Lewis, his head bent toward hers as they talked. Angel wore a robe over her flashy stage outfit. The scene had a feel of intimacy to it, like Angel and Dylan were old friends or romantically involved. Shannon clicked off the phone. No other security personnel patrolled the area.

When Dylan saw Shannon, his hand jerked protectively up to Angel's shoulder. Shannon waved. Dylan lifted his hand in greeting. Still, he displayed that look of guilt. Angel waved back as recognition crossed her face. It seemed like eons ago a much quieter-looking Angel had stood at her booth and had expressed a desire to come to her shop. Dylan wrapped an arm around Angel and led her around to the back of the stage out of sight. Clearly, he didn't want to talk to Shannon or have her strike up a conversation with Angel.

Shannon turned to go, shoving her hands in the pockets of her coat. A sharp chill hung in the air. Wind blew loose food wrappers and fliers across the empty park like paper tumbleweeds. She should go home. Deborah might have hot soup waiting for her.

Still feeling stirred up by her conversation with Sissy, Shannon knew she wouldn't be able to settle down if she went home. She thought about calling one of the Purls to see if they wanted to get together for late-night cocoa. Maybe she could phone Betty and talk to her about what she'd learned about Helen. Or she might swing by Michael's office, and with any luck, find him hunched over his desk. *He might have let his phone go to voice mail because he's working.* When she checked her watch, it was nearly eleven o'clock. Who was she kidding? She wouldn't find anyone awake at this hour.

Shannon stood in front of the darkened windows of the Paisley Craft Market. She knew she wouldn't feel sleepy for hours. She unlocked the door to the shop and stepped inside. She was positive she could find tasks to do in the shop to burn off some of her nervous energy. Perhaps working would settle her racing thoughts.

She clicked on the lights and watched as one section after another of the store became illuminated. Focusing all her energy on Betty's workshops and the booth meant she'd neglected other things. As she walked around the shop, her soft-soled shoes padding lightly, she saw that most of the displays could use some straightening. She started with the jewelry-making area where the strings of beads looked like they'd been hit by a hurricane.

As she worked, she thought she heard the floor above her creak. She froze, her thoughts immediately returning to Marilyn's murderer. *Don't do this to yourself. It's probably the wind. This is an old building; it creaks.* Hearing nothing more, she took a deep breath and moved on to the scrapbooking section of the store, which was in worse shape than the beads.

She got into a rhythm as she straightened the loose paper. Focusing on a physical job usually calmed her. The silence of the shop helped too. When her phone buzzed in her pocket, she was startled, and a piece of scrapbook paper drifted to the floor. Shannon pulled her phone out. Michael's name and number flashed on the screen. He'd sent a text message:

"Please meet me at the warehouse. I think I've found something. Michael."

— 17 —

Shannon gripped the phone in her hand. Michael had grown curious about the circumstances of Marilyn's death as well. Had he gone ahead and checked into Sissy's background? Maybe he was helping the police with something. Grayson might have shared the forensics report with him.

She quickly turned out the lights and stepped out onto the street, deciding it would be easier to walk the short distance rather than get Deborah's car. The warehouse wasn't too far from the town center, on a short little spur of a street. All the downtown shops were closed, their windows dark. She passed only two other people before she turned onto the street which led to the warehouse.

Shannon stood before the large front doors of the warehouse. No police tape hung across the door. *Grayson must have finished with any official business he needed to do.* She looked around for Michael and tried the doorknob. As expected, it was unlocked. She pulled open the door and stepped inside, fumbling unsuccessfully along the wall for a light switch.

"Michael?"

Shannon stepped deeper inside the building, running her hand along the rough textured walls until she finally found a light switch and clicked it on. In addition to Melanie's Apple Queen float, two others occupied the large room.

Turning slightly, she scanned the entire room.

This doesn't feel right.

"Michael?" She turned back toward the door to leave. The metal of the warehouse made an odd creaking sound. As her hand reached out toward the doorknob, her cellphone rang. She jumped as if she'd been shot.

She pulled the phone out of her purse and stared at the unfamiliar number. "Hello?"

Michael's voice came across the line. "I got your message about Sissy and—"

Dread pooled in Shannon's stomach. "Why are you calling me from this number?"

"I misplaced my phone right after I saw your message."

Shannon fumbled for the door as a rising sense of panic invaded her awareness. "Why aren't you at the warehouse?"

Michael paused before answering. He spoke in a measured tone as though Shannon were a child. "Why would I be at the warehouse?"

A hand covered Shannon's mouth. She dropped her phone in an attempt to get away from her assailant. She freed herself long enough to scream and prayed the phone was still transmitting. *Please let Michael hear me!*

The man grabbed her again. He slipped a cloth bag over her head so she couldn't see.

With his arms clamped around her torso, holding her arms in place, he dragged her across the floor. She twisted one way and then the other, unable to free herself from his iron grip. He kicked open a door with a loud boom. Her feet dug furrows through the gravel as he dragged her across what she thought must be a parking lot. No matter how much she resisted, she couldn't get away. She tried to take a deep breath, but instead sucked in a mouthful of the fabric covering her head. It took all of her strength not to panic.

She heard a screeching sound and felt herself being lifted sideways. Then the strong arms released her, and she dropped a short distance. She felt industrial carpet beneath her and smelled oil. Yanking the pillowcase off her head, she had enough time to see the trunk lid of a car slam down over her.

She blinked rapidly as her eyes adjusted to the darkness.

She struggled to get a deep breath, banging on the trunk lid. "Help, somebody! Let me out of here!"

Footsteps crunched on gravel, and then the car started up, swaying as it gained momentum.

She balled her hand into a fist, hitting the underside of the trunk lid several more times. She shouted until her voice grew hoarse. The car sped up. *No one will hear me now. Time to come up with a new strategy.*

Shannon felt around in the darkness. Her fingers found a crowbar in the corner but not much else. *Where is he taking me?* It had clearly been a man who had grabbed her in the warehouse—her theory about Sissy proven wrong. Sissy demonstrated a compulsive stealing habit, nothing more.

The car gained more speed. They were likely on the highway. Her attacker must be intent on killing her, probably taking her to a place where her body would never be found. Shannon shivered, struggling to stave off the fear which made it hard to think straight.

Whoever he was, he'd made a serious mistake by not checking the trunk thoroughly for a makeshift weapon. Shannon gripped the crowbar tightly. When the man opened the trunk, she'd be ready to use it. The car rolled along, the sound of the surf rising above the rumbling engine noise. She almost could taste salt in the air as she mulled over how she'd been deceived.

She'd sent the message to Michael. He'd gotten it and looked into Sissy's background. But he'd called from a different phone. Someone must have taken his phone shortly after he'd received her voicemail. Dylan would have access to his phone. *Could he be the mastermind Jason Lynch took orders from? How could he fool someone like Michael?* Perhaps Dylan had played the "I'm like the son you never had" angle so well that Michael hadn't done his usual deep background check.

Shannon held the crowbar tightly even as her legs cramped. Her knees were pressed into her stomach, allowing very little room to move. None of what she had discovered would matter if she didn't get out of the trunk alive. Working with Michael gave Dylan the excuse he needed to be in Apple Grove. Maybe that look of guilt he always displayed was because he knew she had a vested interest in finding out how the scam had been committed against Betty.

The car slowed as the road changed from pavement to gravel, and the wheels rolled to a stop.

A door slammed.

Shannon adjusted the crow bar in her sweaty hands, waiting for her chance to strike.

Footsteps crunched on rocks. She held her breath. The smell of the ocean wafted in to her tight space. No one came.

She waited. Tense silence fueled her anxiety.

What is he doing? It doesn't take that long to walk around to the back of a car.

She heard voices. Shouting. Something thudded against

the car, shaking it over and over. The noise of a struggle, or maybe her assailant lifting a heavy object, pressed on her ears. She couldn't tell. Another object thudded against the car and then more silence.

To keep her mind occupied and prevent her fear from getting the best of her, Shannon counted the seconds. She heard more voices, this time calmer. Someone fumbled with the lock on the trunk. It sprung open as moonlight flooded in. Dylan Manion stood above her. He tilted his head and grinned down at her.

"Take this, you creep!" Shannon swung the crowbar, hitting him hard on his upper arm. Dylan's eyes grew wide as he reeled backward. Unfolding herself, she crawled out of the trunk and lifted the crowbar to strike again. Someone grabbed her from behind.

She turned to push the second man off. "Don't touch me!"

"Shannon. It's me. It's OK."

"Michael?" She blinked. "Michael! You came! But how—" Her voice cracked.

"It's all right. You're safe." Michael reached out for the crowbar and tossed it to the ground.

"No! It's not OK!" Shannon whirled to face Dylan. "We can't let *him* get away."

Dylan held up his hands. "I'm not going anywhere. I'm only doing what the boss asked me to do." He stepped to one side, revealing another man laying facedown in the sand, his hands tied behind his back.

Jason Lynch.

Shannon couldn't compute what she was seeing. "But I would have smelled him."

Jason raised his head. "They make us take showers in jail, lady." He spat out the words.

She recalled the large bottle of cologne she'd seen in his hotel room. Of course he wouldn't have access to it. "The whole medical scare was an act," she stated.

"So he could plan his escape," Michael said. "It's much easier to break out of a hospital than a jail."

Shannon nodded as things started to make sense. "The only one who'd said there was a mastermind was Jason. He lied to throw me off his trail."

"And the only one who could keep me in jail was you." Jason's voice took on a bitter tone.

Dylan brushed sand off his arms and looked at Shannon. "None of this explains why you tried to crush my skull with a crowbar."

Shannon rushed toward Dylan. "I'm so sorry. Every time I saw you, you acted so ... guilty."

Dylan grinned and shook his head. "I'm twenty-five years old. I've done a tour of duty in Iraq, and I have security qualifications that would impress the FBI, Mrs. McClain. But every time you look at me, I feel like I'm ten years old again, and my mom caught me with my hand in the cookie jar. Nobody else can do that to me."

Shannon could feel the heat rising up in her cheeks. "I didn't mean to make you feel like that."

Michael stood beside Shannon, placing a hand on her shoulder. "Shannon is a very perceptive person. She's good at seeing through a person's veneer. I can understand why you felt that way."

"I still don't understand why you did things to make

yourself look so suspicious," Shannon said. "That's why I was doubtful in the first place. I mean, checking the security of a supply closet at the inn? What kind of a story is that?"

Dylan closed the trunk on Jason's car and then looked over at Michael. "Can we tell her now?"

In the distance, sirens sounded, and Jason groaned in protest.

Michael turned to face Shannon. "I hired Dylan because there's a leak on my security team."

She blinked. "What are you talking about?"

"We deal with a lot of high-level people in government, entertainment, and corporations. Little secrets about them, ones that only a security team member would know, were appearing in the press," Michael said.

Dylan moved toward Jason.

Michael continued, "So with Angel Lewis's cooperation, we created different rumors about her and fed them to individual members of the team to see which one leaked out."

That explained why Dylan was looking so cozy with her after the concert. She remembered Michael telling her about Angel Lewis's check bouncing and wondered if it was part of the ruse, which would mean that Michael lied to her also. "Was one of the rumors that Angel Lewis was in financial trouble?"

"No," Michael said. "We got that straightened out with her accountant. She did take out a big chunk of cash and not tell anyone."

Shannon was relieved Michael hadn't lied to her as part of his internal investigation. The pieces still weren't all fitting together though. She turned back toward Dylan. "But what were you doing up in the supply closet at The Apple Grove Inn that day?"

"One of the other employees took a phone call. I wanted to listen through the wall from a place where he wouldn't be aware of me, to see if he let anything slip about another client."

The sirens grew louder as Dylan hauled Jason to his feet, his features still contorted in a tight ball of anger.

Shannon walked toward him. Though the deception about a mastermind had worked to throw her off, in some ways Jason wasn't very smart. "Why didn't you just get a room at the inn and sneak into the office to find out that personal stuff?"

Jason turned his head to the side, refusing to make eye contact. "They were booked full up for the stupid festival. I told Marilyn we should come some other time, but it had to be this weekend for her. She insisted."

Shannon angled her head around, forcing Jason to look at her. "How did you know Marilyn Seagrave?"

Jason bared his teeth. "Quit asking me questions! I demand a lawyer."

Clearly, he wasn't going to confess to killing Marilyn. "The police will figure it out sooner or later, and they'll know if you had anything to do with her death."

Jason snarled at her.

The police SUV pulled off the road, and Chief Grayson emerged from the driver's side. He took in the scene. "Glad to see everybody is OK here."

Officer Brownley opened the passenger-side door, ambled over to where everyone stood, and handcuffed Jason.

"Jason escaped from the hospital as the concert ended,"

Grayson said. "He sure didn't waste time getting into more trouble."

"That reminds me." Michael walked over to Jason and dug in his shirt pocket, pulling out a phone. "He must have taken it right after I checked my messages and saw the one from Shannon. I set it down on a speaker."

Jason sneered. "I needed the phone." He looked at Shannon with hate-filled eyes. "Lucky me, it had your contact information in it."

Shannon turned to address Michael. "So you were still at the park when I called?"

Michael nodded. "I was in a car, questioning the employee who we were pretty sure leaked the secrets. I couldn't answer my phone."

"It's been a long day and night for everyone." Grayson hooked his thumbs on the police belt that surrounded his ample middle. "Why don't the three of you come by tomorrow, and we'll take your statements. Shannon, do you need a ride into town?"

"She can ride with us," said Michael.

Shannon looked up into Michael's shining blue eyes. "You're OK with that?"

Michael shrugged, an indent forming between his eyes. "Sure. Why wouldn't I be?"

"You seemed pretty upset when I suggested Dylan was up to something. I thought you were mad at me for questioning your ability to do background checks." Shannon walked beside Michael.

Michael reached over to open the passenger-side door for her. "Your comment made me afraid the cover would be blown. If you thought Dylan was up to something, then maybe the other members of my team would be suspicious too." Michael gazed at Shannon with admiration in his eyes. "The rest of my team isn't quite as good at reading people as you are. I'm sorry if I came across a little harsh."

"Apology accepted." Shannon settled into the car.

Dylan slipped into the backseat as Michael started the engine. He turned the wheel and pulled onto the highway.

Dylan leaned forward, resting his arm on the front seat. "We never would have known how to track you down if Michael hadn't called you back about your message and you mentioned being at the warehouse. We saw Jason's car speed off when we arrived and followed it."

Shannon nodded solemnly. She might be dead and buried by now if not for that one bit of fortunate timing. "God does have a way of protecting us sometimes, doesn't He?"

"I did a cursory background check on Sissy O'Connor," Michael said. "She was arrested once for shoplifting. Nothing else."

Shannon felt heaviness in her heart for Kristin. Would talking to Sissy make a difference? She'd become instantly defensive that Shannon had surmised there was more going on besides shoplifting.

Michael caught up to the police car. Shannon could see the outline of Jason's head as he turned to look out the back window.

"He certainly threw me off by telling us there was someone else setting everything up," Shannon said, almost in a whisper. "We still don't know for sure who killed Marilyn—

or why. And after everything that's happened, Betty still doesn't have her sister back."

Michael gripped the steering wheel a little tighter as compassion flooded his voice. "Yes, your friend has been through the emotional ringer." His voice had a faraway quality to it. "She lost and found and then lost a sister."

"Grayson will probably have a confession out of Lynch by tomorrow morning," said Dylan.

Shannon stared out the window. "I hope so."

Who else would have motive for killing Marilyn? No one else in town knew who she really was.

They drew near to the outskirts of Apple Grove. The police SUV turned off the road toward the station, and Michael drove through downtown, past the town square. The remnants of the festival were still in place, a few empty booths and tents and the giant banner which read "Welcome to Apple Grove."

"It must be nearly one o'clock in the morning," Shannon said as the car passed darkened windows and empty streets.

"Do you have a way to get home?"

"I left Deborah's car by the shop," Shannon said.

Michael rolled down the street until he came to the Paisley Craft Market storefront.

"Thanks," Shannon said. "You saved my life tonight, quite literally."

Michael offered her a warm smile. "All in a day's work."

He'd gone above and beyond for her. Her heart filled with gratitude toward him. "Listen, I'm pretty wound up. I don't know if I'll ever sleep. Would you guys like to join me in the shop? I can fix us some tea."

"Actually, I have something I need to get done," Michael said. His expression gave away nothing, as though a veil had fallen over his features.

Shannon arched a brow. "This late?"

"It's a bit of research which can't wait until morning."

And he clearly wasn't going to tell her what it was. Feeling a little hurt that he'd declined her invitation, Shannon opened her door. "In that case, I should probably go home too."

"I'll wait until you are safely in the car before I go," Michael said.

"Thanks." Shannon slid out of the passenger seat. Dylan pushed open the back door and took her place in the front seat.

What could Michael possibly have to do at this late hour that couldn't wait until tomorrow? She slipped into Deborah's car and turned the key in the ignition, eager to share the news with her friends about catching Jason Lynch. But it would have to wait until tomorrow. No one else would be up at this hour.

She took the winding road up to the Paisley estate. By the time she pulled into her circular driveway, the need for sleep had finally kicked in. The porch light burned bright as she trudged up the stone steps to the front door. She entered a silent house and noticed the light on the land-line answering machine blinking, but she decided she'd deal with it in the morning.

Once in her bedroom, Shannon kicked off her shoes and slipped under her comforter, fully clothed. Her last thought as she drifted off to sleep was of Marilyn.

Why had Marilyn insisted they run their scam on this particular week?

— 18 —

The next morning, Shannon found Deborah in the breakfast nook, sipping her coffee. She grabbed a bag of English Breakfast tea and put the kettle on to boil.

"There's some sausage and scrambled eggs in the refrigerator, if you want to heat them up," Deborah said.

"Thanks." The store didn't open until one on Sunday. A slow morning and late church service sounded luxurious.

"Melanie called while you were still sleeping. She wanted to know if you could get together at the craft market before it opened. She said she'd swing around to pick up Betty."

So much for a leisurely morning.

"Sure, I can do that." Shannon opened the refrigerator and pulled out the eggs and sausage. "I'll give her a call after I eat."

"Say, you kept busy night last night while the rest of us slept." Deborah pushed the newspaper toward her.

Shannon picked it up. Page one was all about the festival and Angel Lewis's appearance. The bottom half of the page read "Apple Grove Burglar Caught." Her eyes widened at the four-inch story about Jason Lynch's arrest and her role in it. *The reporter must have been listening to the police scanner and interviewed Grayson.* Jason was believed to have worked at the halfway house where Marilyn Seagrave was a parolee.

The article didn't say anything about Jason confessing to her murder. "It was nice of Grayson to mention my name."

The kettle whistled, and Shannon pulled it off the burner. After pouring the water, she dipped her tea bag in a mug.

"The man from the body shop brought your truck back yesterday. He put it in the garage." Deborah flipped idly through the newspaper classifieds.

Shannon pulled the reheated breakfast out of the microwave. "I bet you'll be glad to have your car back."

"I don't leave the house much anyway," said Deborah. "I didn't mind loaning it to you."

After Shannon finished her breakfast, she called Melanie and made plans to meet at the shop in twenty minutes.

When Shannon stepped into the garage, the sight of Old Blue was a welcome one, like seeing a good friend. Old Blue put up her usual fight before chugging to a sputtering start. She loved the boiling bubbling sounds the old Ford's engine made.

She pulled out of the garage. Deborah's car looked so small and forlorn in the huge circular driveway. She hadn't had the energy to put the car in the garage last night. Beth's truck seemed to fit the hugeness of the driveway much better. Shannon let out a breath. *Beth.* With all the excitement, she'd forgotten that she still hadn't found out why her mother left early—that was the only assumption which made sense at this point. If Beth was still around Apple Grove, she surely would have caught up with Shannon by now.

As she drove down the road into town, Shannon decided her mother would call her at some point with an explanation as to why she'd left town earlier than expected. When she pulled up to the Paisley Craft Market, the interior lights were already on. No surprise there. Melanie had an extra key since she sometimes took early shifts at the store.

Shannon opened the door and prepared herself for an onslaught of questions from the other Purls. When she rounded the corner to where Melanie, Kate, Joyce, and Betty sat with their chairs in a circle, she found each of them already busy working on a craft.

"Well hello there, junior crime fighter." Joyce winked at Shannon.

"So I guess you've heard," Shannon said.

"Do they know yet if Jason Lynch is the one who killed Marilyn?" Betty asked. She stopped knitting for a moment to glance up at Shannon.

Shannon sat down. "He's the most likely candidate, but he hasn't confessed." She told them about the conversation she'd overheard when Marilyn was talking on a cellphone and it sounded like she was getting cold feet.

Melanie worked her needle through a cross-stitch project. "Those were her exact words—'it's all too much for me'?"

Shannon nodded. "Yes. At first I thought she meant being with Betty was too much for her emotionally, but now I think she wanted to back out of the scam."

"What I don't understand is that they knew about the inn five years ago. Why wait until now to come to Apple Grove?" Joyce asked, knitting with eyelash yarn in a bright shade of pink that matched her signature color lipstick.

Melanie furrowed her brows. "That is strange, isn't it?" She wound the same piece of thread around her finger several times, not making much progress on her project.

"Maybe they thought everyone would be so busy with Apple Festival stuff, it would be easier to pull things off," Kate said.

Shannon sorted through her bag of potential knitting projects, listening to everything that was being said. Was it coincidental that Marilyn and Jason had rolled into town during the Apple Festival? "Betty, did Marilyn say anything which might have implied she wanted to stay long term?"

Betty looked up from her knitting, the clicking of her needles slowed. "She hinted that she didn't have a lot of money or much of a life in Portland." Her knitting stopped altogether. "I assumed because she was my sister, we would have lots of visits together." Her eyes shrouded in sadness.

"Coming only for the Apple Festival wouldn't make sense if they planned to run the scam over a period of months or even years," Shannon said.

Melanie shrugged. "Maybe it was just a coincidence that they showed up this weekend."

"I don't think so." Shannon recalled what Jason had said. "Marilyn specifically wanted to come here this weekend."

A gentle tapping at the front door drew their attention away from their conversation. When Shannon rounded the corner, she saw Michael standing at the front door. She unlocked it, and poked her head out. "Michael?"

"Deborah said I'd find you here. Why don't you and the ladies come outside and stand out on the sidewalk?" Michael beamed, excitement in his voice.

"Huh?"

"I have something I want all of you to see."

Shannon studied him. *What exactly is he up to?*

He leaned toward her, his blue eyes dancing. "Trust me, it'll be good."

"*All* of us need to come out?"

Michael checked his watch and glanced down the street. "Yup."

"OK. Give me a minute." Shannon closed the door and returned to the circle of women. "Ladies, I have a request from Michael that we all go stand on the sidewalk. He has a surprise for us."

"Oh, I love surprises!" exclaimed Joyce, tossing her knitting aside.

Kate arched a brow. "The surprise is on the sidewalk?"

Melanie rose from her chair, placing her cross-stitch to one side. "I'm game. It could be fun."

"Why not?" Betty set down her knitting. "But I'm only agreeing because it's Michael."

Shannon laughed. "I'm warning you, I have no idea what he's up to."

As they moved toward the door, Melanie linked her arm through Shannon's. The five of them stood on the nearly empty sidewalk outside the shop. Just another Sunday morning in Apple Grove. The bookstore and grocery wouldn't open up until the afternoon. A handful of people, whose faces looked familiar even if Shannon couldn't remember their names, meandered down the walk.

Michael stood beside Shannon, checking his watch and gazing out into the street.

"So have you heard anything from Chief Grayson?" Shannon asked, shoving her hands into the pockets of her cardigan. If they had to wait much longer, she might need her coat. "Has Jason confessed to the murder?"

"I talked briefly to Grayson when I went in to give my statement. Lynch has confessed to the scam, but he isn't giving up anything else. He asked why they think he would kill the goose which was about to lay the golden egg," Michael said.

"It's a good question. He couldn't run the scam without Marilyn. But I think she wanted out," Shannon said. "Who else had motive to kill her? Nobody else in town knew who she really was."

Michael opened his mouth, about to answer her question, but just then, a car pulled up beside the Paisley Craft Market. Dylan pushed open the driver's-side door. He glanced in Michael's direction, a conspiratorial look passing between them.

Michael gave him a nod, and Dylan opened the passenger-side door of the car.

As the door opened, Michael said, "Ladies, I'd like you to meet the real Helen Cline."

— 19 —

At the sight of the real Helen Cline, all five of the women gasped in unison.

Betty touched her hand to her face, shaking her head. "I don't believe it." She looked over at Michael with a questioning glance.

"It's all been verified and thoroughly checked out." Michael couldn't stop smiling. "It's really her."

The tall older woman stood for a moment, taking in her surroundings. She clutched her purse close to her body, and her gaze landed on the five women.

Betty burst over to her and wrapped her arms around the woman, crying and gushing, "Oh, Helen! I can't believe it's you."

Shannon turned toward Michael, gazing at him with admiration. "So finding the real Helen was what you had to work on so late last night."

Michael lifted his chin. "It only took a little bit of digging. You have to know where to look."

"You are full of surprises, Michael Stone."

The real Helen was tall and slender like her younger sister. The scar that ran from her ear to her mouth had faded over time, but it was still visible. Her dark brown eyes glazed with tears when she looked at Betty.

"Everyone," said Betty, "I'd like you to meet my older sister, Helen."

All the women offered warm greetings.

Helen lifted her eyes to the Paisley Craft Market sign. "What a wonderful place this must be."

"We hear you're quite a quilter," Melanie said.

"Why don't we all go inside? We can get Helen something to eat and have a visit," Shannon suggested.

Helen turned to face her sister. "I'd like that."

The women flowed through the doors. Shannon glanced over her shoulder, expecting to see Michael, but he was already gone.

They visited in the coffee shop for over an hour. Helen filled them in on her side of the story. She had only a vague memory of Jason Lynch working at the halfway house. People had often referred to Helen and Marilyn as "the twins" because they looked so much alike. She confided in Marilyn about Betty, not comprehending what Marilyn would do with the information. Marilyn had gained Helen's confidence by talking about a late-in-life child she'd given up for adoption and talked about searching for. Helen didn't know if the story was true or not.

Helen took the initial steps to find Betty and learned about Tom and the inn, but then she became afraid too much time had passed and lost her courage to get in touch. Helen now lived in a small town in central Oregon only about four hours from Apple Grove.

The women talked and laughed until it was obvious Helen was getting tired. Apparently, once Michael had located Helen, Dylan had driven all night to get her and bring her to Apple Grove.

With her face beaming, Betty leaned close to her sister.

"We have so much catching up to do, and I have the perfect place for you to find rest."

"I'm looking forward to seeing more of that beautiful inn of yours," Helen said.

The sisters left, and gradually the other Purls said their goodbyes. Shannon stood alone in the quiet store, thankful Betty's emotional roller coaster ride ended well.

She gathered up the tea mugs and took them to the sink. The shop didn't open up for another hour, but the front door bell jangled. Shannon realized she hadn't locked it after the women left. She rounded the corner from the coffee area. "Sorry, we're not open—"

Kristin and her mother stood at the entrance.

"I wasn't expecting you to come in today," Shannon said.

Kristin looked toward Sissy. "My mom has decided to get help for her problem."

Sissy stepped forward. "After you came by last night, I was angry because I was pretty sure you were going to … I was afraid you had found out about the merchandise missing from the store."

Kristin took her mother's hand in her own.

"I thought Kristin would lose her job because of me, that you would fire Kristin for stealing. I would never do anything to hurt my daughter." Sissy's voice faltered. "But then I finally realized I *have* been hurting her all along."

Shannon's heart swelled. "Well now, that is good to hear."

"Thanks for everything, Mrs. McClain," Kristin said.

Shannon nodded. "You know anytime the store gets busy again, you'll be the first person I call."

"Thanks. We just stopped by because we thought you should know."

"I'm glad you did."

Both women slipped out. After locking the door, Shannon returned to the sink to rinse the used cups and place them in the dishwasher. She straightened up the area where the Purls and Helen had visited. Then she headed back to the main part of the store to make sure everything was ready for opening.

A woman in a dark coat with a scarf around her head tapped on the window.

Shannon unlocked the door and opened it. "I'm sorry, but we don't open for another half hour."

"I saw a light on and thought you might be here," said the woman. She acted like she knew Shannon. "I only have a little time before I have to leave town." The woman slipped her scarf off, revealing dark hair.

Shannon studied the woman closer. "Angel?"

Angel Lewis looked very different without all of her makeup and brightly colored clothes—more like when Shannon had first met her. Without the long fake lashes and pink streaks in her hair, she appeared downright mousy. Even her demeanor seemed dialed down from her onstage persona. Now she understood what the singer had meant by being able to "fade into a crowd" without being recognized.

Shannon smiled. "I suppose I can make an exception." She opened the door a little wider, and Angel stepped inside.

"Your shop sounded so wonderful that I had to come to see it." Angel did a half turn around the shop. "You said something about silk fabric for pillows?"

Shannon led Angel over to the fabric section of the store. "You have an abundance of choices."

Angel brushed her hand over the fabric. "So beautiful." She unbuttoned her long blue coat. "It's hot in here."

"I can take your coat." Shannon grabbed the coat and placed it on the counter. She turned back around to face Angel, who wore a brown dress with a gathered skirt.

"You have so much stuff in here." Angel wandered toward the jewelry-making section. "Do you have charms? One of mine fell off. I don't know where I lost it." She turned her forearm toward Shannon, displaying the bracelet.

Shannon stared at Angel's drab outfit and then at the bracelet.

Angel looked at her. "Something wrong?"

A revelation clicked in Shannon's brain. Joyce had mentioned seeing a woman in a brown dress running toward the woods the day Marilyn died. "You've worn that dress before."

Angel drew a hand to her cheek and shrugged. "I don't take that many everyday clothes with me. Most of the suitcase space is for stage costumes and interview outfits."

Shannon stepped toward her. "You wore it the day of the bad rainstorm in the park."

Angel let the strand of beads she held drop from her hands as her forehead wrinkled with confusion. She spoke slowly. "Yes ... what are you getting at?"

"And that bracelet." Shannon pointed to Angel's wrist. "Was it a little silver teddy bear charm you lost?"

Angel's eyes grew wide as she touched her wrist. She tilted her head. "Did you find my charm?"

All the pieces fell together. Joyce had said she'd seen

a woman in a brown dress running toward the trees. Angel had been abandoned by her mother at the age of six. Marilyn connected with Helen by telling her about the daughter she'd given up.

"All this time," Shannon said, "I thought this was only about stealing. But it was also about reuniting."

Angel gripped the neckline of her dress. "What are you talking about?"

Shannon spoke slowly and deliberately as a complete picture formed in her mind. "Marilyn chose to come here during the festival because she knew you would be here." Ads had been run for months and for miles outside of Apple Grove. "You met her in the woods the day of the rainstorm. The day she was ..."

The color drained from Angel's face. She took a step back, shaking her head. "It's not what you think."

"But she *was* your mother."

Angel slowly nodded. "She didn't want me. She never wanted me ... not even now that I'm famous. Like that should've made a difference." Her voice faltered. "She only got in touch with me because she wanted my money."

That explained the unexpected drain on Angel's account. "You followed her into the trees."

Angel reached out a hand for a shelf, seeking support. Her voice grew thick with emotion. "I hated myself for thinking I could buy my mother's love. Being rejected by your mother is a hole in your heart nothing can fill."

"It's a terrible thing to have a mother who hurts you like that. I would understand your rage," Shannon pressed. Was it possible that the reason Marilyn had been killed had nothing to do with the scam? *Did Angel kill her mother?*

Angel planted her feet. "I followed her when she ran toward the trees. That much is true. I was mad that she'd manipulated me. But I saw matters clearly by then."

Instinct told Shannon that Angel was telling the truth. "So what happened?"

"I heard the struggle. I saw a man shove my mother into a car and drive away. She'd dropped her purse. I took it because I wanted the money back. I gave her cash. She doesn't even have a bank account."

Shannon spoke gently. The poor girl had been through so much. "Angel, why didn't you go to the police?"

"I was ashamed, and I didn't want the scandal. One hit song doesn't mean you have it made for life." Angel lifted her head even as tears formed in her eyes. "I don't want people's pity. I don't want them to treat me like the poor little orphan girl."

"But you saw the man who shoved her in the car." *Marilyn hadn't been killed and then moved. She might have died in the warehouse.*

Angel's eyes glazed with tears. "You have no idea how much she hurt me and kept hurting me. I didn't care if they caught her killer."

Shannon placed a hand on her shoulder. "I understand why you would feel that way. I need to know if you got a look at the man who pushed her into the car."

Angel took in a ragged breath and wiped her eyes. She seemed to relax a little. "They argued for a moment. I couldn't hear all of the conversation. Marilyn said she had enough money. Then she said something about quitting or not wanting to do what they had planned—she didn't want to go back to jail."

So Marilyn had wanted to back out—but not because she felt guilty about ripping off Betty. Instead, she'd chosen the less risky path of shaking down her daughter. "Angel, this is very important. Tell me everything you remember about the man."

Angel nodded. "Dark, curly hair. Medium build. Leather jacket."

Jason Lynch. "Angel, you have to go to the police. Only you can identify your mother's killer."

Angel took a step back, the look of resolve on her face unchanging.

"I'll go with you," Shannon urged. "We'll try our best to keep your name out of the news."

Angel squared her shoulders and looked at the floor. "No."

"I know your mother was not a good person, but you still have to do the right thing. Jason has not confessed. You are the only one who can bring him to justice. Without your testimony, he'll get away with murder."

None of what Shannon said seemed to sway Angel.

Shannon continued, "It's quite possible he'll come after you at some point if he thinks you can identify him. I know from experience that's how he operates."

"After me?" Angel's eyes still glazed with tears. "I suppose you're right."

Shannon held out her elbow for Angel to wrap her arms through. "I'll stay with you the whole time if you need me to."

Angel wove her arm through Shannon's. "Thank you."

Shannon took Angel to the station and waited with her while she identified Jason Lynch as the man who had pushed Marilyn into the car.

"You'll have to come back for the trial," Grayson said to Angel as he closed out the computer file on her statement.

Angel tensed and twisted the tissue she'd been holding.

Shannon sat next to Angel in front of Grayson's desk. "Chief, is there any way we can keep Angel's name out of the press?"

"The issue about Angel giving her money won't be part of the trial," Grayson said. "But we need her to testify that she saw Jason force Marilyn into the car. We'll do everything we can to keep it low-key until trial."

"Thanks." Angel pushed back her chair. Turning to Shannon, she said, "I'll call one of the band members to pick me up. I have a rehearsal in Portland I'm going to be late for."

Shannon offered Angel a hug. "You'll have to come back to Apple Grove when you're not so busy. I'm sure we can get you interested in even more crafts."

"It's a deal," said Angel.

— 20 —

Shannon stepped outside to the police station parking lot. A car had pulled up to where Angel stood waiting. A man with blond and purple hair got out and ran around to open Angel's door. She waved goodbye to Shannon before getting in.

When Shannon returned to the craft market, she found Beth's car—not the Gourmet on the Go truck—parked in front of it on the street. Beth stood on the sidewalk.

Shannon smiled. "Somehow I knew you'd show up sooner or later."

"You looked like you were deep in thought."

"I was thinking about something Deborah said. She said family can be the greatest source of joy and the greatest source of pain." Shannon now realized it was so true, not only for Betty, but for Angel too, and for Kristin.

Beth rubbed her chin and looked off into the distance before answering. "Deborah has always been wise about things like that."

"Where have you been? I thought you were taking off after the concert."

"Didn't you get my message?"

"Your message?" Shannon asked, pushing open the shop door and stepping inside. Essie already stood poised for business behind the counter.

Beth followed Shannon inside. "There was no answer

on your cell when I tried. I called your home phone, thinking you'd be more likely to get that message."

Shannon's cellphone was probably still on the warehouse floor. She had a faint memory of the flashing light on the answering machine at home. "Oh! Sorry. I ran pretty much all day and all night."

"Me too. On impulse, I went back to Portland and put out the fires I needed to put out with my employees instead of sticking around for the concert," Beth said. "I don't talk on the phone while I'm driving, and by the time I got to Portland, you weren't picking up."

"Why the change of plans?"

"Actually, I remembered Monday was your day off." Beth's eyes twinkled.

"Yes, it is."

"I thought I'd help you out in the shop today and maybe tomorrow we could spend the day together without any distractions."

"I think that sounds wonderful, but let's start the visit today." Shannon tilted her head toward Essie. "Do you mind going solo today?"

"We won't be busy," Essie said. "Go enjoy yourself."

Beth brushed a strand of hair off Shannon's face. "So, catch me up. Why have you been running a hundred miles an hour?"

Shannon opened the door to the shop. "Tell you what. Let's head home, and I'll fill you in."

Shannon wrapped her arm around her mother, and the two women stepped outside into the crisp fall afternoon surrounded by the quiet autumn beauty of Apple Grove.

Turn the page for an exclusive preview
of the next mystery in the
Creative Woman Mysteries series.

Deadliest in Show

COMING SOON!

— 1 —

"I would kill to have talent like yours!"

Shannon McClain smiled at the group of women who gathered around the displays at her table, admiring her handcrafted jewelry. They'd been at her booth at the art and craft show for the past twenty-five minutes, going back and forth on which necklace and bracelet they each should purchase. For a moment—just a moment—Shannon felt like a celebrity as they gushed over her work.

She came back down to earth long enough to give a reasonable response to their sweet comments. "Well, it's part talent and part hard work, but thank you. I'll take the compliments." Her Scottish accent lilted with each word.

Shannon had to admit that she loved hearing the fuss over her creations. She'd worked hard to develop her jewelry, and it was nice to see the payoff. Since she sold much of her jewelry online, she didn't always get to see her customers' faces light up with admiration.

She'd spent the past several weeks designing elegant jewelry to sell at the first ever West Coast Art and Fine Craft Festival. Everyone in Apple Grove had been delighted when their city had been chosen out of several in Washington and Oregon to host the prestigious show, organized by the Artists Guild of the Northwest.

A three-day event, it was taking place in the local high

school gym, which was packed with exhibitors who displayed only high-quality work. But the gym was also packed with customers hoping to get an early start on their Christmas shopping—or at least that's what several people had told Shannon.

There was so much competition to get into the show. Only the best of the best had been chosen by the jury who'd overseen the application process. Shannon could see why. The Guild had done a great job of advertising, and people from up and down the coast had traveled to attend the event.

The three women at her booth, who said they'd driven down from Portland, finally picked the items they wanted and paid. They walked away happy customers, which made Shannon one happy jewelry maker.

"You've had no shortage of compliments over your work." The voice beside Shannon startled her.

Sunny Davis, whose adjacent booth featured her stained glass art, had slipped up beside Shannon as she served customers. Shannon and Sunny had chatted quite a bit on Thursday in between customers, and Shannon felt like the two were kindred spirits.

"I certainly can't complain. Nor can you, apparently." Shannon nodded toward Sunny's booth, where half of her beautiful masterpieces had already been purchased. "It looks like you're going to sell out."

Sunny glanced down at her table. "I like doing shows like these. They remind me of my roots. This is where it all started for me."

Shannon pointed to the magazine article displayed on Sunny's table. *The Artist's Touch* was one of the top arts-

and-crafts magazines in the country, and the cover featured Sunny. "It certainly doesn't appear that someone of your caliber would need to do a craft show to promote your work."

Sunny sipped from her bottle of flavored water. "You do some things out of logic. Other things you do from your heart. These shows help feed my heart, if you know what I mean."

"I understand. My friends convinced me to apply for the show. When I was accepted, I decided I'd donate my profits to a local charity. It seemed like a win-win situation that way." Shannon's friends in the Purls of Hope knitting club had also agreed to help her out during the show so she wouldn't have to man her booth alone.

Sunny's eyes lit up. "What a great idea! I'll have to do that the next time someone asks me to enter a show." Her hands went to her hips. "Better yet, maybe we could plan a whole show where *all* profits go to a charity. Wouldn't that be fun?"

Shannon had to agree. "That sounds like a fabulous idea."

"Let's exchange cards and talk about it sometime after this weekend."

"It's a deal."

A group of women meandering to her booth pulled Sunny away from the friendly exchange, and Shannon turned away just in time to see a familiar figure approach her table.

"If it isn't Shannon McClain."

Michael Stone stopped at her table and fingered a leaf-print necklace with a casual grin on his face. He watched her, the detective in him easily trumping his friendly demeanor. He was always observing, always taking mental notes of everything around him. In his forties, with close-cropped black hair, blue eyes, and a six-foot-plus height,

Michael had the rugged good looks of a TV detective—but he was the real deal. He co-owned the private investigation and security consulting firm Stone & McCrary.

Shannon scolded her heart for skipping when their eyes met. She'd accepted the fact that he was romantically off limits. He still had ghosts from his past to make peace with before he'd be ready for another relationship. In her mind, she *knew* this. So why did she react this way whenever she saw the man?

She cleared her throat. "Michael. What a pleasure. I didn't see you as an art show kind of guy."

He shrugged, his overcoat damp from the drizzle outside. "I was out and about, and decided to see what everyone's making such a big fuss over. This show is all I keep hearing about around town."

She spread her arms out as if displaying the entire showcase floor like a game show hostess. "Well, things are sure hopping. There is indeed reason for all the fuss."

Shannon's gaze traveled upward until it met Michael's again. His piercing blue eyes were perceptive and breathtakingly beautiful. But they weren't hers to stare at. They were just friends, and it was better that way. "So what really brings you out this way?" she asked.

"I'm on my way home from a job. I just happened to be passing by." His eyes twinkled. "I thought I'd stop and say hello."

"Well, I appreciate the gesture. Have you walked around yet?" She nodded toward the rest of the showroom floor, where forty of the region's best had their work displayed.

"I saw you when I walked in and came right over. Your

booth is hard to miss, and I didn't give the others much more than a glance."

"You're right. I couldn't have asked for better placement." Truly, she'd gotten a great spot, not very far from the entrance where almost all the show's guests were certain to walk past. "Would you care to stroll around a bit?"

He smiled. "With you? Yes, I'd love to."

Shannon saw her friend Joyce Buchanan walking toward her with a steaming cup of coffee in hand and waved. Joyce's wide grin nearly matched the sparkling beads on her shirt. Bedazzling was her newest favorite thing to do, and not one clothing item or accessory seemed to go untouched. A member of the Purls of Hope, Joyce was in her mid-forties; she had platinum blond hair and a full figure. She was also a member of the local artists guild. Though she was volunteering for the entire show, Shannon felt fortunate to get most of her attention. Shannon knew that Joyce didn't take time away from her bakery, Pink Sprinkles, very often, but she'd lined up assistants at the shop to help out during the art show this weekend.

"Am I ever glad to see you."

"Who isn't?" Joyce asked with a grin and an exaggerated poof of her hair.

"Precisely. But I do have ulterior motives. Do you think you could watch my booth for a moment? I'd like to stretch my legs a bit."

Joyce winked. "Sure thing."

Shannon joined Michael on the glossy wooden floor of the gym. They stopped almost immediately to admire Sunny's work. She had made gorgeous light catchers to hang in windows, as well as lampshades and night-lights. Sunny was helping a customer, so Shannon simply waved.

"I'll introduce you to Sunny later. She's the sweetest lady," Shannon told Michael. "We're lucky to have such a high-profile artist at the show."

Michael peered closer at one of the items on the table. "One of those lamps might look good in my office. What do you think?"

Shannon felt flattered he'd asked her opinion. Usually he avoided anything that hinted that their relationship might be anything but professional. They had had only one date, and that had almost ended in disaster. Since then, their interactions had been, at best, awkward. "I think you're right," she agreed. "That would look lovely."

"Hey, Shannon." Sunny stepped closer as her customer left. "Stretching your legs for a bit?"

"I have trouble sitting still for too long."

Sunny grinned. "I understand that." She extended her hand toward Michael. "Sunny Davis."

"Michael Stone. Nice to meet you. Your work is beautiful."

"Thanks." She rubbed her temples. "I'm hoping I'll be able to make the entire show this weekend."

"Is something wrong?" Shannon asked.

She shook her head. "Just a headache. Maybe a bug. It seems to happen every year at this time—with the seasons changing and all. Perhaps I need to start taking vitamins to boost my immune system."

Shannon nodded. "Drink lots of orange juice too."

As another customer approached, Shannon and Michael excused themselves and continued their walk around the gym.

"So, the show is going well?" Michael asked as they jostled through the crowds.

"There are some great artists here—some of the best on the West Coast, if not in the nation. The level of craftsmanship is outstanding. I'm honored to be a part of it."

"I'm just glad that you're doing this instead of being caught up in solving some crime." He offered a wry smile.

Shannon couldn't resist a playful elbow to his side. "You do realize that I don't *look* for mysteries to solve, right? They seem to find me."

He frowned. "That's what worries me."

"*I* worry you?" She watched his expression with a strange sense of amusement.

"I don't want to see you get hurt."

The sincerity in his eyes caused her heart to do an inadvertent flip.

She cleared her throat. "I appreciate that."

A balding man who stood a couple inches shorter than Shannon stopped in front of them. He had his smartphone in hand and an air of briskness about him. "Are you Shannon McClain?"

"I am." Shannon didn't recognize the man, so she regarded him cautiously.

He extended his free hand. "I'm Rupert Murphy, and I'm the president of R & M Designs. I've had my eye on your work for awhile now."

R & M Designs was one of the premier jewelry companies in the country. Their unique pieces were found in jewelry stores in malls from the Pacific to the Atlantic. Shannon grasped his hand, and he pumped it briefly. "I'm honored that you've even heard of me," she said.

He glanced at his phone before sliding it into his pocket and putting his hands on his hips. "I've been studying your designs, and your work is really outstanding. Your pieces have a unique touch that sets them apart from others."

"Thank you. I appreciate that." Pride surged in her. She'd put a lot of work into her jewelry, and it was lovely to be noticed.

"I'd like to talk to you sometime when you have a free minute and things aren't so hectic."

"If you don't mind me asking—about what?" She couldn't even begin to fathom where he might be going with this. Perhaps it had something to do with her business, the Paisley Craft Market & Artist Lofts.

The man's lip curled into a half smile. "About coming to work for me."

"Coming to work for *you*?" Shannon's heart stuttered a beat, noticeable enough that she raised her hand to cover her chest. "Wow. I'm flattered."

He handed her a business card and peered at her through his bushy eyebrows. "Call me. I can make you a really nice offer that would get you out of this little rinky-dink town. We can have your work in all of my stores nationwide. I can make you a household name."

Shannon opened her mouth, ready to defend Apple Grove, but before she could respond, Rupert slipped back into the crowd. She stared at his card a moment before stuffing it into the back pocket of her jeans. When she looked up, she saw Michael studying her.

"Sounds like you're about to hit it big time. Even *I've*

heard of R & M Designs, and I'm by no means a jewelry guy." Admiration shone in his gaze.

She blinked, still in shock over the brief conversation. "I don't know. That was so unexpected. I don't even know what to think."

"Sounds like a once-in-a-lifetime opportunity. You should call him. It's about time someone recognized your talent. You do a lot for other people. You should consider doing something for yourself."

"But he mentioned something about leaving Apple Grove. Why would I want to do that? I love it here ..." She shook her head and began walking again. "I've got to let that sink in some more. Besides, I don't want to jump to conclusions. I haven't even heard everything he has to say yet."

As they walked past a table displaying homemade candles, the fragrances of cinnamon and lilacs wafted up. Scents were in abundance at the show, from candles and handcrafted soaps and lotions to the food court catered by a local restaurant in town that was known for its soups.

Shannon's stomach rumbled at the thought of food. Lunch remained a couple of hours away, and she regretted her meager breakfast now. She should have packed some apple slices or a granola bar.

Pausing in front of a woodcarver's booth—a man who did beautiful scroll-saw work on a variety of items including room dividers, wall hangings, and Christmas ornaments—Shannon couldn't help but overhear the conversation between him and the show organizer, Mark Arnold. Shannon had heard Mark was a real stickler for details. In her brief interactions with him, Mark's prickly ways hinted at a perfectionist personality.

That could work well for running a business, but not so well for interpersonal relationships.

Michael leaned closer. "That looks like a heated exchange."

Shannon nodded, uncomfortable that the two men were arguing in public. "Not sure that will serve as the best publicity for the show. You can teach a lot of things, but you can't teach people skills."

"I can't argue with that."

"Shannon!"

Shannon turned her head toward the sound. *Who now?* These shows were like reunions for all the artsy residents in the community, including the people who often shopped in Shannon's store.

She looked around and spotted Hunter Banks standing a short distance away, looking a little damp from the rainy weather. Hunter was a marine biologist who had come to town a few months earlier. He was tall with sandy hair, deeply tanned skin, and green eyes that sparkled with life. His gaze left hers and locked with Michael's.

Tension stretched between the two men like wire between two highline poles.

It *must be my imagination*, she thought. It had to be. Michael hadn't expressed any intentions toward her besides friendship for a while now. And although the attention from Hunter felt flattering, she wasn't a schoolgirl prone to crushes. She considered herself a professional woman who remained in total control of her emotions.

Most of the time.

She cleared her throat. "Good to see you, Hunter. What an unexpected surprise."

He returned his focus to Shannon and grinned. "I didn't want to miss the opportunity to see my favorite girl."

Shannon nodded toward the aisle in front of them. "We were just walking around and enjoying some of the work here. Would you care to join us?"

"I'd love to."

As the three began to walk, with Shannon sandwiched in the middle, she couldn't ignore the awkwardness of the situation. What exactly could she talk about with these two men simultaneously, other than the weather or football? Her idea of football was what they would call soccer, and neither had admitted to being a soccer fan. So the conversation seemed destined to be about the dreary weather. After they'd discussed it at length, they all fell silent.

Michael cleared his throat before nodding toward the food court. "How about I go get us some coffee?"

"That sounds great," Shannon agreed quickly. "Could you check and see if they have tea? Earl Grey?"

He smiled. "Of course." His grin slipped as he turned toward Hunter. "And you? Would you care for anything?"

Hunter shook his head, droplets of water from the rain outside dripping onto his jacket as his eyes danced with ... was it amusement? "I'm good. Drank a thermos of coffee on my way here."

Michael mumbled something and slipped away, leaving Hunter and Shannon to peruse the aisles of handcrafts alone. Hunter picked up a hand-painted ostrich egg. "Impressive."

"And expensive." She pointed to the price tag. "Be careful with that."

His eyebrows shot up, and he set it back down carefully. "Noted. I had no idea eggs were so expensive."

They braved the jostling crowds again, pausing to note various pieces of art. Finally, Hunter turned toward her and spoke. "So, I have an ulterior motive for stopping by today."

"Do you?"

"Yes, I hoped maybe we could go to dinner sometime this week." He paused. "What do you think?"

Shannon was so accustomed to Michael keeping his distance that hearing someone actually be forward about his intentions threw her off kilter. Despite that, her first instinct was to say no. However, her friends in the Purls had scolded her often of late about not giving anyone a chance. Perhaps it was time to push herself outside her comfort zone.

She smiled, though it felt forced. "I'd love to. Why don't I call you when I have my calendar nearby, and we'll confirm a time and date?"

"That sounds perfect." He glanced at his watch. "Look, I've gotta run. I just wanted to catch you here and see your beautiful face for a moment."

He was quite the charmer, Shannon had to admit. His attention was sweet and flattering, and it added a dose of excitement to her life.

In a great twist of timing, Hunter slipped away just as Michael appeared with her steaming cup of tea.

"He sure left quickly." Michael watched him leave and took a sip of his hot coffee. Black, Shannon had no doubt. He was a no-frills kind of guy.

She shrugged. "I guess he didn't have much time."

"Interesting." Michael turned toward her. "I hate to

abandon you also, but I need to get going. Maybe we'll catch up over coffee and tea another time?"

Shannon smiled. "I'd like that." She raised her cup. "And thanks for the drink."

"Anytime, Shannon."

She was still smiling when she returned to her booth.

Joyce raised her eyebrows, her gaze following Michael in the distance. Shannon had no doubt her friend had seen the whole exchange.

"I do believe that you have two men vying for your attention," Joyce said.

Shannon flicked her hand in the air, setting her sterling silver bracelets jangling. "Nonsense. They're both just friends."

Joyce chuckled, shaking her head. "Men like Michael and Hunter do not stop by craft shows just for the fun of it." She pulled out a powder compact and a tube of lipstick and began to reapply her trademark fuchsia color to her lips. "You're beautiful and smart and creative, and those men have obviously noticed that."

Shannon started to speak, but stopped. She had no idea how to argue with a compliment like that, so she decided that she wouldn't. "Let's just concentrate on the show. It's like the Super Bowl of crafters. I'd rather not waste our time talking about men."

"Two handsome men, I should add." Joyce wagged her eyebrows and grinned.

Shannon laughed at her friend's silly antics before letting her gaze peruse the showroom floor again. There appeared to be a lot of happy customers wandering about, talking to the various exhibitors.

Her gaze stopped at her neighbor. She squinted when she saw Sunny. The woman's head rested on the table atop one of her stained glass windows. Shannon's heart raced at the sight. The woman had mentioned not feeling well earlier, but Shannon had no idea she'd felt this miserable. She should go home and have someone else man her booth if she felt this bad.

"Sunny?" Shannon rounded her table and approached Sunny's.

The woman remained still. Shannon gently reached forward and gently nudged her shoulder. "Sunny?"

Still no movement.

Shannon nudged her harder, and Sunny tumbled to the floor. Shannon didn't have to feel for her pulse to know the woman was dead.